They had drawn close together as if for protection; outside the fence Reidel had seen last night a long low car had drawn to a stop and a man was walking across the fields toward them.

Reidel said, "You'll have to handle this, Mathis," and thrust the telempath forward . . . after a moment Mathis answered the stranger in his own language. The others listened, but only Cleta understood.

When Mathis had finished speaking to the stranger, he said in under-toned Dvanethy dialect, "He doesn't believe me. But he's going to take us—just Reidel and me—to a city near here. Wait here for us . . ."

The telempath touched Reidel's wrist, and Reidel heard, like a voice inside his brain, the clear-cut command.

Get one of the shockers. Keep it out of sight. Find some way to slip it to me . . . He thinks—I can't quite make it out—that for some complex reason we are pretending all this—For these people belief that humans live on other worlds is a form of insanity.

Books by Marion Zimmer Bradley

ENDLESS UNIVERSE
THE FALCONS OF NARABEDLA
SEVEN FROM THE STARS

The Darkover *Series*

THE BLOODY SUN
THE PLANET SAVERS
STAR OF DANGER
THE SWORD OF ALDONES
THE WINDS OF DARKOVER
THE WORLD WRECKERS

From Ace Science Fiction

SF

Seven from the Stars

Marion Zimmer Bradley

SF
ace books
A Division of Charter Communications Inc.
A GROSSET & DUNLAP COMPANY
51 Madison Avenue
New York, New York 10010

SEVEN FROM THE STARS

Copyright © 1962 by Ace Books, Inc.

An ACE Book

Cover art by Steve Hickman

4 6 8 0 9 7 5 3
Manufactured in the United States of America

Seven from the Stars

SPECIAL BULLETIN: Released from News Service of Galactic Center, received at Dvaneth.

The starship *Northwind*, carrying colonists to an isolated sun in the Spiral Arm, has imploded.

The Master Panel, which carries sensitive studs corresponding to the self-destroying implosion units installed, for obvious reasons, in all spacecraft, confirmed today that the implosion device of the *Northwind* has gone dead.

Cause of the disaster is unknown. It is surmised that the *Northwind* may have been surprised and threatened with capture by Rhu'inn-dominated ships, and that the crew may have activated the implosion to prevent ship and passengers from falling into Rhu'inn hands.

The exact position of the *Northwind* at the time of her destruction has not been ascertained. No noticeable mass disturbance on energy detectors has been reported from any inhabited planet. It is probable that the *Northwind* had deviated considerably from her computed course in an attempt to avoid capture, and perhaps strayed into the Closed Planets.

The escape of any survivors is unlikely. Lifeships are not released prior to implosion unless a planet is detected within lifeship range. The swift death of implosion is more merciful for possible survivors than a lingering death drifting in interstellar space. There are relatively few stars in that section of the Spiral Arm, and of these only a fraction are possessed of habitable planets. The probability that the *Northwind's* lifeships may have been released in the vicinity of any of these planets is astronomically small.

The crew and passengers of the *Northwind* must for all practical purposes be considered legally dead.

1

"GET CLEAR, get clear," Reidel shouted, "the units are set to go off almost at once after we surface! Grab the kits and run, but get clear!"

Still dazed with the long agony of deceleration from interstellar space, the handful of survivors stumbled down the steps of the lifeship which, like the mother ship, carried a self-destroying mechanism set to implode upon surfacing, unless set in place before landing by a crew member.

They got their first look at one another in that moment when they emerged into glaring, yellow sunlight and dusty, windswept space. They didn't waste time looking. They fled, scattering like seed blown by intangible disaster, across sandy wasteland that seemed to heave and sway under their groping feet. Behind Reidel one of the women caught her foot, twisted her ankle and fell heavily to the sand. Reidel, not urgently but with desperate haste, picked her up and shoved her along.

"This is far enough," Reidel shouted. "Lie flat! Get down!" Glancing back over his shoulder, he saw the little ship for the first and last time, still glowing red from their brief searing trip through atmosphere.

The old man collapsed, rather than fell, and Reidel bent over him, thrusting a hand into the neck of his shirt. His hand came away reddened. The tall woman dropped to her knees beside them.

"Is he—dead?" she faltered.

"Not quite."

The others had thrown themselves flat in the sand, and Reidel could hear one of them still crying in convulsive spasms. The tall woman alone stood, like a frozen statue, staring at the red pulse of the ship. Reidel, straightening from the old man's inert body, was gripped by the intense fear in her eyes; he too gazed, almost tranced, at the glowing, pulsating ruby shimmer.

Then the crimson frame buckled and with a slow, almost lazy grace, erupted skyward. Shouting, Reidel threw himself forward, dragging the woman roughly down. The blast of sound and the thundering inrush of tormented air rocked the desert, while the units vibrated, fragmentized, vaporized, atomized. A crimson glow lingered where the ship had been; it wavered, drifted and was gone.

On the sand of the alien world nothing remained but a little heavy, dark-reddish dust, unscattered by the wind.

"Well," said Reidel, in a curious flat voice, "that is most emphatically *that*."

Letting the woman fall, tumbled and passive, from his arms, he rose and looked around.

A flat and sandy wasteland stretched away to a horizon of low hills, speckled with a blackish mottling of small shrubs. In the sand around them dry and bunchy grass grew sparsely in clumps, dried out by long drought. There were some prickly bushes and low, leafless trees, stunted and twisted and blackened. Reidel scowled at the bleak scene. A small, thorny plant grew near him; he bent and touched it with a curious finger, and a drop of blood appeared on the ball of his finger. The leaf was sharp as a needle.

At one edge of the sky a yellow-red sun was either rising or setting. In the flurry of the automatic landing there had been no chance to determine the period of the planet's rotation, or indeed anything about it except that it was habitable. If the ship's automatic meters had not registered a range of temperature and atmosphere that could sustain human life, the meters themselves would have locked the implosion units before landing. And then they would have died very quickly and mercifully and without knowing they were going to die.

But habitable? That could mean anything from the icy deserts of Rigel II to the searing jungles of Vialles—or anything in between!

It was cold, or seemed so to the Dvanethy. A brisk and scentless wind, laden with little gritty swirls of dust, blew restlessly around them. The sky was an ugly bluish-brown, dimmed to a dusty haze near the horizon, and through this dust the sun was a bloody inflamed eye.

Reidel looked around again, automatically counting the survivors. Most of them were strangers. Reidel's work had kept him too busy for the social life of the passengers. But he knew, vaguely, who they were.

The old man with the smashed chest was Kester; he was some sort of minor official on the ship's staff. They had found him lying, senseless and bleeding, in the lifeship bay, flung there by buckling metal through a gap in the corridor that had not been there seconds before.

The dark slender woman, still stretched out on the sand, was called Cleta; Reidel knew only that she was one of the aristocratic caste of telepaths from Vialles, and even in the crowded society of the spaceship, the Viallan telepaths held themselves haughtily aloof from the rest. Beside her a dark, sturdy boy, just edging out of adolescence, was blinking, half dazed, his head propped in his hands. He was Arran, one of the apprentice engineers in the Rim Room of the starship.

Crouched in a taut huddle, his face hidden, a misshapen dwarf knelt in the sand, oblivious to all but his own agony. He was Mathis—one of the ten telempaths who had been so carefully shielded from contact with the mental babble of the packed humans in the spaceship. Like all his kind he was physically a ruin, warped and hunchbacked, and though young in years, his dark, coarse hair was already streaked with long dashes of white. At his feet a half-grown albino girl, raised herself to her knees, shielding great bruised eyes from the fierce sunlight. Then she struggled to her feet and glanced, just once, at the empty, charred patch where the spaceship had been.

The seventh and last of the survivors, a young woman heavy with child, had been flung senseless on the clumped grass, and still lay there, dazed by the shock wave, not moving. The albino child went slowly toward her, bent, and raised the pregnant girl with gentle hands.

"Here, Linnit," she said in a soft and reedy voice, "have a look at our new home, won't you?"

Then she turned, looking up at Reidel with an appraising stare. She had a childish face and a child's body still immature under a childish smock; but the great eyes were not childish. They were far too wise, too mature, too sad for her few years. She had the freak coloring that marked out the hypersensitive empath, and Reidel shrank before the intense wisdom and compassion in those wide eyes.

She said, "I know you, don't I? You're Reidel. You looked after the animals, didn't you?"

Reidel nodded. Then, aware that he must speak or die of the idiot laughter that bubbled up in him—he had spent so much time and worry, trying to transport those accursed animals across interstellar space in good condition—he said, "I know you, of course, but I've forgotten your name."

"Dionie," the child said. "Do you know all the others?"

The pregnant girl was on her feet now, whimpering, trying to pick the thorns from her hands. Dionie took the torn fingers in hers, gently pulling out the prickers.

"This is Linnit, Reidel, and that's Cleta."

Cleta sat up and flung back her long disheveled hair, flinching when she moved her hand. Arran got up and turned toward Reidel.

"Do you know what happened?"

Reidel shook his head. "No. Don't you? I was off-shift and sleeping, and the alarm bells went off, and the ceiling in my cabin hit the floor, and I decided it was time to get out of there. The next thing I knew, we were all in the lifeship and it was kicking loose."

"I don't know a thing about it," Arran repeated. "They'd been running double shifts in all the drive rooms, but none of the engineers would tell me why."

"I don't suppose it makes a bit of difference," Reidel said at last. "We're here. I don't think any other lifeships got loose, though. Do you know where we are, Arran?"

"Somewhere in the Closed Planets, I suppose."

"What exactly does that mean?" Cleta demanded, in the arrogant tone of a woman used to instant deference.

Reidel's temper was uncertain at the best of times, and now he lost it completely.

"Is this a time for questions? If your brain is so empty it needs something to rattle around, you might start collecting the kits, or look after this man," he indicated the bleeding Kester, "instead of asking stupid questions about Galactic politics!"

"I thought it might help to know exactly what we may be facing," Cleta retorted, "and you seem to be taking charge!"

"If you think you can do better, you're welcome to try! That sun's lower than it was. If it goes down at that rate, it will be dark in a few minutes. We'll have to make a fire, there's no telling how cold it gets here, or—" he paused, deciding there was no sense in mentioning other dangers. "I wonder if these bushes will burn?"

"I'd think so. They're dry enough." Arran studied their black twisted limbs. "Ouch!" He shook his hand and sucked it. "Careful—thorns!"

"Everything we've seen has thorns." Reidel hoped none of them were poisonous and decided not to mention that either. Cleta, moving stiffly, was collecting the survival kits from the lifeship. She knelt to unfasten one, but Reidel's heavy hand fell on her shoulder.

"Leave that for now. You're able-bodied, come and help gathering wood. Fuel's what we need most now."

Cleta shook off his hand and obeyed. Reidel worked in tense haste, dragging heavy dead trees into a little hollow where a ridge of banked sand gave some protection from the cutting wind. Dionie, too frail to lift the branches, raked the dry tumbleweeds together, ignoring their stinging prickers.

The last rim of the sun vanished into a dull twilight. Reidel knelt, trying to make his pocket-flare catch fire, choking on the rank smoke when the dry weeds smoldered for an instant and went out. He crouched, swearing, shielding the flame from the wind with his cupped hands.

In the lee of the piled brushwood, a tiny desolate moan sounded. Cleta, biting her lips against the pain in her wounded hand—a manicure tool had been driven through the palm in the first shock wave that had smashed the passenger deck into rubble—crept around the bushes and found Linnit, curled into a forlorn huddle and wailing softly.

It was not in Cleta's nature to think much about anyone but herself; nor did she now. The weeping lacerated her already torn nerves; she dropped on the ground and snapped, "Stop that! What good does it do?"

Linnit wept. "I wish I were dead!"

"So do I," said Cleta brutally, "you're no help." The cold tone was better than sympathy; Linnit struggled to control her sobs, then twisted in pain and cried out.

"What's the matter?" Cleta asked unsympathetically. "I didn't know you were hurt." Her hand throbbed like searing fire, and she wrung it, softly, to ease the burning pain.

"I don't know—oh, I don't know!" Linnit writhed in uncomprehending torment. Cleta tried to disentangle herself from the strangling clutch of the thin arms, but Linnit gripped at her in frenzied terror, and Cleta could not get away without hurting her.

At last the flames leaped up into the darkness, and Reidel raised himself, stretching cramped and stiffened legs. "Now if the women have those kits ready—" His eyes fell on Cleta, where she knelt beside Linnit.

"What's the matter with her?"

"I don't know, I don't know!"

"You wouldn't know, would you?" Mathis, the telempath, dragged his twisted body from the shadows. His tight smile held a relishing malice, as if he thoroughly enjoyed their ignorance of the situation. "She isn't dying, there's nothing much wrong with her." Seeing that Cleta still did not understand, he added with sarcastic emphasis, "The baby is coming. That's all."

Reidel swore wearily. "As if we hadn't enough trouble without that!"

But the words threw Cleta into shivering panic. "What are we going to do?" she whispered, and let Linnit slide from her lap, drawing away in frightened rejection.

Reidel let himself drop to the ground. The unfamiliar darkness, the foul smoke and the strangers gathered around him, made noisy confusion in his brain. He wished, knowing the futility of it, that Kester had not been hurt. He, Reidel, didn't feel fit to do the thinking for all seven of them. He wished somebody else would speak up, but nobody did.

So he made his voice rude and intentionally harsh.

"Do? Well, we can all sit around and hold a wailing ceremony, or we can calm down and make some sense. Unless women are different from other female animals," he put it as roughly as he could, to shock the women into quiet, "it will be some time before we have to worry about Linnit. Meanwhile, let's think about other essentials. Such as—who's hurt, and how badly, and what's in these so-called survival kits? Maybe in the morning, we'll find out we're safe on a Federation planet, maybe we won't. But for tonight we're on our own. So let's start deciding whether we want to live or die."

It was the longest speech he had ever made in his life.

Dionie began to slit one of the kits with her fingernail. She made a little, surprised sound; there was a whirring noise, and then a taped voice, speaking Standard said, "Attention. You are cautioned to destroy every item in these kits before making contact with populations outside the Dvaneth Federation, unless they are identical with articles of local manufacture. Attention. You are cautioned to destroy—"

Dionie took her hand away and the voice stopped. They crowded around her to see what was going on.

Dionie began to lift out small sealed packages. Not many rations, some pliable sealed flasks—which were labelled WATER. From between the packages she lifted thin folds of all-purpose synthetic fabric—folds and folds of it, compressed to cushion the other articles. It was warm and impervious without being bulky, and could be molded and sealed, without sewing, into any form of garment. And a vagrant ripple quirked the albino girl's mouth.

"Does that warning notice mean that if they wear other kinds of clothing here—or if they don't wear any, we have to go naked too?"

"It means exactly what it says."

The girl looked down at the ground and murmured, "I know. I just thought it was funny."

"I'm glad something's funny," Reidel said without anger.

"They wear clothes," Arran muttered. "It's cold!"

Dionie was still exploring the packet. "A flare. You should have had this when you were trying to make fire, Reidel. A knife, and—what's this thing?"

Reidel turned the gadget over. "Water detector." He poked under the folds of cloth. "Anything more?"

Arran lifted up the last object. "Shocker," he murmured.

Reidel's mouth was grim. "That's in case we meet vicious wild animals—or worse."

"And that's all?" Linnit exclaimed, "and they call it survival? No—no artifacts? Nothing?"

Reidel shook his head. "It's just what it's supposed to be. Never mind the other kits, Dionie, they're all identical. Just enough to permit us to survive for the first few days. After that, we adapt, like it or not. It's a—" he fumbled for words, not articulate in abstract thinking, and Arran said it for him.

"A lifeline of Dvaneth culture would only retard adaptation—serve as a cushion. We'll adapt whether we want to or not. It's part of the conditioning they give colonists, to adapt to whatever they find, and it works for us, too. This is just to keep us alive until that subconscious conditioned reflex takes over, and starts adapting us, changing us to fit the planet. Being at the mercy of the new world forces you to forget about possible help, and go ahead and adapt for survival—"

"And if you're going to die, it doesn't prolong the agony," Mathis finished cruelly. Cleta flinched.

"Reidel, is there any possibility that this is a Federation planet?"

"I'm afraid not. In the whole Spiral Arm there are only a couple of dozen Federation planets. The most we can hope for is that it's a recorded planet, with a Watcher stationed here."

"If there is a Watcher, how do we find him?"

Reidel shook his head, glad they could not see his face in the darkness. "That's another problem we'll have to solve later," he evaded.

Arran paced uneasily in the dark. "The lifeship must have made a track in atmosphere, and the implosion—even primitive people have photon-conversion detectors, don't they?"

Mathis laughed sourly, but Reidel only said "We'll hope so," and began unwrapping a ration packet. "We ought to eat something and rest."

The thin, raucous laughter of the telempath cut the silence again. "Little rest any of us will get tonight—eh, Linnit?"

Reidel sighed. He wished Mathis would shut up. He wished they would all shut up, and let him get his bearings. Kester, on whom they might have relied, was hurt and probably dying; Arran and Dionie were holding up well under the shock, but they were too young to be much help. Already he resented Cleta, and Linnit's whining, sorry as he felt for the girl, rubbed his nerves raw. And Mathis, who should have helped, was making matters worse with his jeers. Maybe he should have left everything to Mathis from the beginning. But he wasn't used to telempaths.

Most of the races called human are telepathic to a greater or lesser degree. But ordinary telepaths receive, and transmit, only worded thoughts. Hence telepathy between different language groups—or even those whose education and environment have given them widely varying sets of semantic value symbols—is almost impossible. A scattered few were like Dionie—empaths, endowed with the ability to pick up the emotions and sensations of those around them.

The telempath, rarest of human sports, was capable not only of probing the thoughts and emotions of all humans and some nonhumans, but of translating these alien concepts into the language and concepts of any other race.

They had been bred originally for work among the nonhuman Rhu'inn; but that was long ago, while the Federation still had some hopes of peacefully resolving the Rhu'inn menace. That experiment had failed, but the telempaths remained. A rare few of them were used for contact with the inhabitants of alien planets and for other purposes. Their main characteristic was a fantastic degree of adaptability. Their powers were legendary.

Reidel had never seen one before. They lived in strict seclusion. He thought abruptly, *I can see why*. Mathis certainly wasn't the type to win any popularity contests!

Dionie and Arran were trying to make Kester comfortable on a length of the cloth. Reidel wondered if they should move him, then abandoned that line of thought in despair. If he was as badly hurt as that, nothing they did could either help or hurt.

"No, you can't help him," Mathis said to Reidel in an undertone. "He's bleeding inside the skull, too. He's going to die."

Reidel turned away and flung more of the piled wood on the fire. The pungent smoke stung his eyes and he covered them with his hands, trying to hold back a strangling cough. The loss of the ship, the deaths, the long sustained suspense of escape had the numbing quality of a nightmare, and now it was as if he woke out of it and found the nightmare was real.

He hardly knew it when Dionie put food into his hands, though he accepted it, thanking her with automatic courtesy. But he did not put it to his lips, and after a few minutes of staring into the fire he felt a small hand slip through his arm and he looked down, startled, into the pale upturned face.

"Please try to eat something, Reidel. You've been trying to make us be sensible. You've got to be strong for us all."

Reidel smiled, but it only stretched his mouth. "I'm not the hero type," he said, but he broke a piece from the tasteless emergency ration and chewed on it.

Near the fire, Cleta, sitting on the edge of the blanket, was coaxing the reluctant Linnit to swallow a few mouthfuls. Her own face bore a look of

patient exasperation that would have amused
Reidel, if anything could have amused him now.

Of all the times for Linnit's baby to be born!
Reidel, accustomed to being around animals,
knew perfectly well that such things didn't wait
on anyone's convenience, but it was a complica-
tion. He wondered if either Cleta or Dionie had the
least notion what to do for Linnit.

He supposed these things came naturally to
women. They'd have to do the best they could.

The process of adaptation had not yet begun;
Reidel was still very much a man of Dvaneth, and
it never crossed his mind to question the custom
of his home planet, which left such things to
women. Looking up, his mouth full, he met
Mathis' inscrutable eyes and wondered if the
telempath read his thoughts, and if so, why he
didn't say something helpful.

He swallowed the last crumb of the food, sipped
a mouthful of water, then turned and looked out
over the distant wasteland. As far as the eye could
see, nothing; nothing but blackness and blank-
ness, shadowy trees, queer rustles and chirps in
the unfamiliar night. A few stars sprinkled the
dark sky in unfamiliar patterns. A dull, misty-
white streak, the Galactic Arm, proclaimed their
distance from Dvaneth. Their home planet was in
the very center of the Arm, and the Dvaneth sky
was ablaze with millions of suns that made the
night brighter than day. The faint, faraway
twinkle filled Reidel with a terrible sense of isolation.

"Reidel—?"

The man turned, realizing that he had come
some distance from the fire. "I'm here, Arran," he
said. But he couldn't go back yet to listen to Lin-

nit's whimpers and Mathis' jeers, and think of ways to turn aside Cleta's barbed scorn. He needed a minute to himself before shouldering them all again. "We shouldn't both leave the women at once."

"Mathis will look after them, better than I could. Let me come with you, Reidel."

Reidel suddenly knew what was in Arran's mind, and was outraged that it should have occurred to either of them. Anger chilled his voice.

"I'm not going to desert the rest of you. I want to climb one of these little hills, and see if I can make out anything on the horizon that looks like a light, a beacon, a city—any place where humans might live."

Arran sounded ashamed. "I didn't really think—"

"I know that. Go back, now. I'll be back in a few minutes."

"Want my flash?" Arran extended a small hand-light, but Reidel refused it. "It would only blind me."

"Right." Arran went back toward the fire, and Reidel walked on, accustoming his muscles to the feel of the firm soil under his feet, the pull of a planet's gravity again. Once he put his foot on some small live thing that scurried away into the grass, and once he scratched his hand on a thorn. Abruptly his stride was broken, and he recoiled, the breath knocked out of him; he had blundered against something in the dark.

Recovering his balance, he stretched out a cautious hand. A wire, about as thick as the seam in his clothing, was stretched taut breast-high in front of him.

Now, faced with the tangible evidence of intelligent life—for wires did not stretch themselves across barren fields—he wished for Arran's refused light. A more impulsive man would have shouted to his companions, but Reidel decided to explore before raising or shattering their hopes.

He followed the wire by touch. It was barbed, and without electrical charge, and was nailed into a rough-surfaced post. On a hunch he ran his hands down the post. It was a fence of four wires, spaced just far enough apart that Reidel could wriggle through if he wanted to. He hesitated, not sure that he did want to.

The planet was obviously inhabited, but by what? The fact of a fence postulated intelligence and something to be kept in, or kept out. It seemed to him that the absence of electrical charge on the wires indicated a low level of civilization. He wished he were the kind of thinker who could accurately deduce the level of a culture from a single artifact.

With sudden decision he bent and stuck one leg through the fence, hauling the rest of his body after it. A low ditch, waterless, bordered the fence; he crossed it and came up on a flat hard surface. Surprised at the change of texture under his feet, he bent and felt it. Some hard, non-metallic substance, too smooth for natural rock—a road? He was about to scramble back and yell to Arran for the light when a pair of distant lights struck across his eyes.

Yellow, spaced about the span of his two arms from one another, they swung up noisily over the horizon, throwing a beam almost to Reidel's feet, and roared toward him at incredible speed. Reidel sprang back, throwing himself flat in the ditch, hoping to be unobserved by the monster machine.

In the fan of light he made out a metal hull, four humming wheels, then the lights flashed past and through glass panes Reidel saw two unmistakably human heads. Reidel lay flat until the last ruby twinkle vanished behind a rise in the road. Then, spent with emotion, he picked himself up. A *human world, then.* And the thing was neither monster nor robot, but simply a surface vehicle of some sort.

Someone screamed his name and Reidel clambered hastily through the fence and hurried back toward the fire. "All right," he called. "I'm here!"

Dionie flung herself upon him. "Oh, we heard it roaring—we saw the lights—" Her thin arms gripped him with terrified force. He let her cling to him for a moment, then guided her steps in the darkness.

"There, there, Dionie. It was only a car of some sort. There were men inside."

"Oh—" suddenly aware and shy again, she pulled away from him. Cleta and Arran flung expectant questions at Reidel, and he recounted his adventure.

"They didn't see me. I hid in the ditch."

"Why didn't you signal them? They might have been able to help us."

"I didn't know who, or what, they were."

Cleta said in chilly sarcasm, "How very cautious of you," and turned away. Reidel, noticing some constraint in her movement, reached out and caught her arm. She tried to pull away, but he drew her into the firelight and with strong fingers turned over her wrist and unclosed her hand. The palm was clotted with dried blood.

"Why didn't you show me this before?"

Cleta was trembling with rage. "You were too busy ordering us around."

Reidel frowned. "How did you do it?"

"A—a manicure knife went through my hand when—when the alarm sounded. It's nothing, I'll look after it."

Reidel paid no attention, motioning to Arran to hold a light close. "Don't be foolish. If any of the tendons are cut, you'll have trouble." He probed and examined it with meticulous care. It was beneath Cleta's dignity to struggle; she curled her lip and said, "You seem to know a great deal. Who do you think you are?"

"Does that hurt?" He bent one of her fingers. "I've had four hundred assorted animals under my care since we left Dvaneth. If we'd reached the colony, I'd have stood in for the medical officer when he was busy." He was annoyed at himself because he bothered to explain. Cleta shrugged and suffered his attentions, and when Reidel had done all he could, which wasn't much, she remarked scornfully, "I hope there are no alien bacteria or fungus here. These important survival kits didn't include medical supplies."

"Short-sighted of them, wasn't it?" said Reidel wearily.

"No, far-sighted," Mathis murmured. "Survival of the strong. Anyone who isn't, is supposed to die in a hurry and be off the other's hands."

Reidel swung round and said through clenched teeth, "If you have any more disgusting ideas, keep them to yourself, will you?"

Linnit made a stifled sound; Cleta turned to rejoin her, but Reidel held her for an additional minute. "Can you manage?"

Cleta's thin shoulders went up and down. "I'll have to, unless—you say the planet's inhabited by men. Kester's dying, and Linnit—needs help. If humans live here—"

"There's nothing I can do in the dark."

"But what are we going to *do*?" Cleta sounded desperate. "We can't just—just sit here and *wait*, can we?"

"Until daylight," Reidel said, trying to summon authority, "that is just exactly what we are going to do."

Arran's voice suddenly cracked. "But we don't even know how long the nights are! If we wait for that sun to come up again, we may sit here until we die! Anything's better than just—just waiting!"

Suddenly they were all raging at him. Cleta shrieked, "We'll die here; I think you want us to sit here and die!"

Reidel took one step toward the girl, his hand lifted to strike her, but he caught himself just before the blow landed, and only grabbed her arm with heavy fingers and roared, "Hold your noise! If you go into hysterics, I'll choke you!" Linnit began to cry again, in noisy childish sobs, and Cleta struggled wildly, clawing at Reidel's set face. Arran came and flung restraining arms around Reidel, and Reidel, his wrath diverted, whirled and caught the boy in a hard blow across the face. Arran, springing aside, eluded the main force of the blow and swung open-handed, the force of his slap sending Reidel reeling.

Reidel clenched his fists and squared away. If they were going to fight, they'd settle it now.

Suddenly Dionie cried out and dropped to her knees. "Mathis! Oh, what's the matter?" she begged, "Look what you've done, you fools, you fools!"

The telempath was sprawled sidewise, eyes closed. "You brutal idiots," Dionie wept, "why do you think the telempaths are kept in such isolation? You've thrown him into shock with your fighting and shouting. Maybe you've killed him! Don't stand there staring, get me some water!"

Shocked into soberness, Arran did as she asked. The collapse of the dwarf had cooled Reidel's rage like a flood of ice. Cleta, her tall tense body trembling, went silently toward the darkness where Linnit lay; Reidel started to follow, but the woman spun around in passionate defiance.

"Have the decency to stay away!"

"I didn't realize—" Reidel averted his eyes from Linnit. "Can I do anything to help?"

"You men had better go around to the other side of the fire," Cleta directed. Reidel lingered, though Arran had already lifted the half-conscious Mathis and was carrying him to a sheltered place. "Cleta—"

"Will you go?" she flung at him shrilly, and Reidel went.

The night grew chilly. The men waited, shivering. After a time Linnit's soft whimpers deepened to a steady moaning. Later Dionie, whiter than when the lifeship blew, came around the fire and dropped in a shaking heap, her face in her hands. To Reidel's concerned question she muttered, "I'm no good, a freakish coward—and Cleta knows—she knew I was—" She muffled her face in her hands, crying silently and miserably. Arran raised his eyebrows and Reidel said tersely, "Empath. She was feeling everything Linnit was."

Arran whistled in dismay.

The fire smoked and blew scattering sparks; heavy damp clouds collected, blotting out the dim stars. Dionie, white and twitching, was really asleep now. After a long time Linnit screamed, and Reidel, starting upright, found himself on his feet and, without really planning it, he strode around the fire.

Cleta gestured him back, outraged. Reidel, though angry at her obtuseness, tried to speak kindly,

"Let me help, Cleta. I probably know more—"

"About animals!" she flung in stinging scorn.

"A woman is an animal," he pointed out gently, keeping his temper on leash. "Cleta, ordinary standards don't apply in an emergency."

"The standards of decency—"

"—decency!" Reidel's phrase was straight from the gutter, and it shocked Cleta into silence. She moved meekly aside and let Reidel take her place.

The fire smoldered to coals. Linnit whimpered now and then, but there was no more screaming; only Reidel's voice, low and reassuring, at long intervals. Mathis crouched apart, his eyes squeezed shut in frantic rejection, trying to shut away what was worse for him than all the rest; the whole interplay of naked emotion from which he had been sheltered all his life. He was like a man brought up in pitch darkness and suddenly dragged into the glare of blinding noon.

On the other side of the fire Reidel covered Linnit and smoothed down her hair—the sort of absent-minded, habitual gesture that he would give any suffering small thing—and looked across at Cleta, smiling. She was wrapping up the baby, awkwardly, like a woman who has never handled one before. She tucked it in beside Linnit, who was already sleeping in exhaustion, and rose to her feet.

"I don't quite know what to say, Reidel, except—I acted like a fool."

"It's all right. I don't think any of us knew what we were doing."

Then Reidel made what he knew, afterward, was the worst blunder of his life. Cleta seemed so frail and gentle, so lovely in her momentary humility, that he could not resist the impulse to put his arms around her and draw her against him. The woman swayed, caught off balance in surprise and momentary yielding, but as his face touched hers she gasped, bringing up her hands quickly to prevent him.

He let her go at once, but the momentum of outrage carried her on, and she struck him hard, across the mouth. "You must be mad!" she said trembling. "Get away from me!"

Before her blazing eyes Reidel knew that if he said anything—above all, any word of apology— it would double his offense. He went like a whipped slave, tasting blood from his broken lip; but his pulse pounded savagely, and it was minutes before he could calm his breathing.

He mended the fire. Kester's body was a long, stark darkness, and Reidel bent over him, not surprised to find that the old man's fluttering breaths had finally ceased.

One dead and one born. They were still seven . . .

He flung himself down, near enough to the fire so that he would know if it died, and closed his eyes.

Search Called Off For Unidentified
Fiery Object

LEVELLAND, TEXAS: Texas Rangers today called off a search for the wreckage of a plane which reportedly crashed over the million acre Branzell ranch late yesterday. The unsuccessful search was called off in the early hours of this morning when the Rangers received formal confirmation from the U.S. Air Force that no commercial, military or private plane had been reported late or missing in the entire area.

A flaming object was observed last evening and reported to the Hockley County police by Edward Marcus, 23, a student at Texas Tech; by his sister, Silvia Marcus, 19, and by Steve Branzell, local rancher and businessman.

Rangers reported that they had found no sign of wreckage or distress flares. The Air Force Base at Lubbock gave an unofficial opinion that the unidentified object might have been an exceptionally large meteor. They offered no other comment at this time.

Miss Marcus, a niece of Branzell, who described the flaming object as "a big red stream of fire" was quoted as saying, "It must have been a flying saucer."

2

THE LIGHT preceded the reddish sun. First the stars went out and the sky lightened from black to blue; then pale sunlight came, and Reidel, who had been lying awake for some time, rose and went to look at Linnit.

The young mother slept heavily, her curly hair tangled around the pretty, sullen face. The baby was only a red wrinkled scrap between muffling folds. Arran asked softly, as Reidel covered them again, "Which?"

"Girl, and they're both all right. Lucky."

"Is it?" Mathis asked without stirring.

Before long, Reidel thought, I'm going to smash that sneer down his throat. He turned his back on the telempath.

"Cleta, wake Linnit up, we've got to talk and make plans."

"Let her sleep, at least," Cleta protested. "She can't—"

"We've all got to get used to doing things we can't." Reidel's voice was grim, but his hands were gentle as he raised the sick girl. "Someone may come here and find us when it's daylight, and we ought to be ready for whatever happens."

Linnit stared around wildly for her baby, then relaxed and leaned trustfully against Reidel's shoulder. The others gathered close. Reidel told them briefly about Kester's death; Dionie sniffled a little, but no one made any audible demonstration. They had all lost too much, too recently, to waste grief on another death, another stranger.

Reidel said concisely, "I don't like speech making. Has anyone any practical suggestions?"

Cleta began, "The car you saw last night. We can't be far from civilization. It might even be a Federation planet."

"It's possible, I suppose," said Reidel. "In that case, of course, they'll have tracked the lifeship and there will already be search parties out looking for us. And, once they find us, we'll be put on the first ship for home. But don't get your hopes up," he pleaded. "It's a very small chance."

"On the other hand," Mathis said, "if the place is inhabited at all, it's sure to be a charted world—"

"Why, then, it's very simple," said Cleta, with a triumphant glare. "We find some center of civilization and ask for the Federation Ambassador."

"And if there isn't one?"

"Then, naturally, we explain who we are and what has happened, and ask for their assistance and hospitality."

"It's not that simple!" Reidel's jaw ridged in sudden anger. "There are a few things you don't understand. We are outside the Dvaneth Federation, and probably on a Closed Planet. And some—in fact, most of the Closed Planets are under domination, or surveillance, by Rhu'inn!"

He paused, reluctant to continue, for Cleta had gone stark white, and even Arran looked frightened.

"That means that any Galactics on this planet wouldn't dare draw attention to themselves. There's probably a Watcher here, but he'll be well camouflaged. It may take us a long time to find him."

"Which means we're on our own," Arran put in.

Reidel nodded. "We'll have to accept what we find here, and live somehow. We'll adapt. We can't help it; we're conditioned to it. We won't have any trouble with language, Dvanethy never do, but otherwise, we're literally starting from nowhere. In one sense, Linnit's baby is the luck- iest of us all."

"Lucky!" Linnit burst into wild laughter, and Reidel stared, wondering if the night's suffering had unhinged her mind. He ignored her; it was the only thing he could do.

"Yes, we were all lucky. The lifeship could have fallen into an ocean. Or at one of the poles, where we'd have frozen to death in the night."

"I wish I had," blurted Linnit. "Why didn't you let me die?" She flung herself away from Reidel, shaking with hysteria. The man felt sick with pity; but he saw Mathis twitch, and he knew that at any cost he must not let Linnit upset them all again. With a movement so harsh and sudden that Dionie gasped, Reidel pulled out the razor-sharp knife he carried and passed it, handle first, to Linnit.

"Go ahead," he said roughly, "cut your throat. One less helpless creature I have to worry about. We'll bury the baby with you, it wouldn't live long with you dead. Well, Linnit, what are you waiting for? Ah, there, there—" as she collapsed in helpless sobs, he drew her close and let her lie weeping, on his shoulder, "I'm sorry I had to do that. It's all right now. It's all right."

Spent and quiet at last, she nestled in the curve of his arm. Cleta's eyes were wide with horror, but Mathis nodded approvingly, and Reidel knew he had passed the only serious challenge to his leadership. He wondered why he bothered.

The sun was up now, and already it was fiercely hot. Reidel said quietly, "We were all accepted as colonists, which means we were chosen and trained for adaptability. There's always a place, on any world, for the adaptable person. We'll manage."

Arran asked, "Do we just sit here and wait for them to find us?"

"Until we know for sure what kind of planet we're on, we don't dare attract any attention. Here's my plan. Mathis and I will go and see if that road leads anywhere. Arran will stay and look after the women. Mathis isn't physically able to go alone; but I don't know the language and I'd be at too much of a disadvantage. We'll come back and report what we find—"

"I don't think we should separate," Linnit faltered. "Suppose you can't get back?"

"There must be some telepaths on this world," Cleta said. "Can't you reach them, Mathis?"

The telempath shook his head. "Not just out of the air like that. Surrounded by a crowd of people of this planet, I could pick out the telepaths, and even make contact with those that weren't. But, not at this distance, not without special apparatus."

Reidel, who was not himself a telepath and knew little about them, lost track of the discussion. He walked away toward the place where the lifeship had imploded. It seemed impossible that there should be nothing left but this little charred patch of burnt-over grass. While the others talked, silently and without drawing attention to himself, he wrapped Kester's stiffening body in a length of the cloth and lifting the frail old man with careful respect, carried him into a thicket.

He stood there for a moment, looking down, wishing he could think of some appropriate way to show respect or indicate the rites he could not, on this strange world, even approximate. Kester had died a long way from home. He bent his head. There seemed a strange, a painful silence around him, and Reidel felt, suddenly, an odd tension. He had been in the presence of death many times; but never like this. His flesh crawled and he stood as if rooted to the spot.

Suddenly he heard Dionie's shrill voice crying, "Reidel!" and the tension broke. Sweating, though it was cold, he found that he could move and run, and he ran back toward the others.

They had drawn close together as if for protection; outside the fence Reidel had seen last night a long low car had drawn to a stop and a man was walking across the fields toward them.

Reidel said, "You'll have to handle this, Mathis," and thrust the telempath forward.

Only Mathis understood the words the stranger called.

"Hello there! Are you folks in trouble?"

Probing, instantaneously, at the stranger's mind for emotional concepts. Translating them into word symbols—and after a moment Mathis answered the stranger in his own language. The others listened, but only Cleta understood.

The stranger was a man about Reidel's age, a husky tall young man dressed in woven brown cloth. His face, sunburnt and peeling a little, was ridged up in skepticism and surprise.

When Mathis had finished speaking to the

stranger, he said in under-toned Dvanethy dialect, "He doesn't believe me. But he's going to take us—just Reidel and me—to a city near here. Wait here for us."

Reidel frowned. "What did you tell him?"

"I told him we'd go. You'll have to trust me, Reidel, or I won't be responsible!" Mathis' words held a trace of menace. The telempath touched Reidel's wrist, and Reidel heard, like a voice inside his brain, the clear-cut command.

Get one of the shockers. Keep it out of sight. Find some way to slip it to me.

Under pretense of bending over the fire, Reidel managed to do as Mathis commanded. The stranger had turned, a little impatiently, toward his car. As they followed, he jerked the door open for them; Mathis clambered awkwardly in. Reidel, unwilling, but not quite ready to risk disobeying the one man of his own race who could find his own way around this strange world, hoisted himself in beside Mathis.

He thinks—I can't quite make it out—that for some complex reason we are pretending all this—

Reidel looked back for a glimpse of the others, but they were already out of sight. He had no idea what Mathis was planning. He didn't much care. He was desperately tired, and he had held up where each of the others had, to some extent, broken. He felt an overwhelming desire to slide down on the comfortable cushions of the car and sleep and sleep. The yellow sun dazzled his eyes, but he jerked himself upright, knowing he must somehow stay alert for whatever Mathis was intending to do.

Mathis stirred; the stranger turned questioning eyes on them that slowly widened into fear—for

Mathis had the shocker in his hand, trained unwaveringly on his temple. The driver twisted in his seat as if to jump at them, but the telempath pressed the control and the man slumped over the wheel. The car came to a wobbling halt.

Reidel looked at Mathis as if the dwarf had suddenly turned into a deadly reptile.

"What have you done?"

"You damnable fool!" Mathis said in disgust. Then, "Sorry, I keep forgetting—you head-blind nontelepaths are the very devil when there's fast action to be taken. He didn't believe what I told him."

"Yet you made us come with him!"

"If I'd used the shocker there, someone would have come along and seen the car. It had to be here, because around this bend—I read him thinking about it—the road turns off on a main highway, and there would have been heavy traffic. We could never have stunned him and escaped."

"You didn't kill him?"

"Hell, no. Shut up a minute, will you?" He bent over the stranger, then straightened, his face white with strain. "I deep-probed him," he said faintly, and drew a long breath. "The shocker will leave amnesia for a little while, but even if he talks about us, no one will believe him. On this planet, as nearly as I can make out, belief that humans live on other worlds is considered a form of insanity." He paused, adding thoughtfully "It's odd, though, that he didn't believe me. I had the impression that he was a telepath."

But Reidel didn't hear. *Belief that humans live on other worlds is a form of insanity.* So there it was. It was a Closed Planet, and there was no hope of rescue. Oddly enough, the knowledge didn't hurt. Hope was what had hurt, and the effort to keep it down to a reasonable level. Now they could forget hopes, and make realistic plans.

"It's our clothing," Mathis muttered. "Nonconformity is dangerous here."

That seemed strange to Reidel who was used to a hundred planetary cultures. But he demurred when, after a moment's concentration, Mathis clambered into the back seat and hauled out a suitcase, flinging it at Reidel.

"There are spare clothes in this."

"We're not thieves!"

"We're safer if he thinks we only meant to rob him."

"You're positive you didn't kill him?"

"No, no, no. This shocker doesn't even have a lethal calibration! Reidel, I'll argue ethics with you all night after we're safe; right now, we've got to survive, even if it means killing him, and if we hang around until he wakes up, we may just have to do that. Get into some of those clothes, you idiot! If someone comes along before we get away, what will happen to the others?"

Convinced, but still unwilling, Reidel scrambled into a spare shirt and trousers he found in the suitcase. They were a fair fit. Mathis was a grotesque figure in the other suit, immensely too large. The dwarf thrust his fingers into the man's pockets and drew out several small items; but Reidel struck them from his hand.

"At that I draw the line!"

Without stopping to argue, Mathis picked them up again. He said grimly, rifling through a rubbed-leather wallet, "Survival. They use negotiable paper here, not credits." He selected, with calm determination, a number of the bills—not all—without looking at their denominations. Then he put the wallet back. He said, "Look at him. He looks well-fed. He has spare clothing. He owns, or has the use of this car. We are not seriously imperiling him. Reidel, I said I'd argue ethics later. Let's get away from here."

Reidel sent a guilty glance backward to the car. "How long will he be unconscious?"

"Not half long enough," Mathis fretted. "By the time the amnesia wears off, and he remembers where he found us—well, by then we had better be somewhere else."

They trudged back along the road for a long time, between plowed fields planted in long rows of brownish shrubs, from which hung fluffy white balls of fiber. Reidel felt heartened. "If they practice agriculture, we won't be completely lost," he said. The desert stretch where they had landed had frightened him more than he knew. Once he grinned in undisguised pleasure, and Mathis, hobbling with his head down, raised bloodshot eyes, blinking dust and sweat. "What are you so happy about?"

"I saw a cow." Mathis scowled scornfully, but Reidel was pleased; where there were cows, there were other animals, and where there were animals, he could find a place for himself.

So far, however, they had seen nothing that could have been a human dwelling place. Reidel was beginning to wonder if they might not have been wiser to take their chances in a city or town with the stranger, when Mathis froze as a rattling roar sounded behind them; a big truck pulled to a stop and from inside someone hailed them.

The telempath listened intently, probing, in that eerie way; then answered in what seemed to

Reidel's keen ear to be yet another alien language. After a brief exchange of words, he said to Reidel, "We can safely go with these people."

Not understanding, but trusting Mathis, he swung himself up over the racks into the back of the truck.

He found himself surrounded by people and miscellaneous possessions that were, as yet, just stacked junk to Reidel. There were several children, a tall girl, an old man. In the truck cab, a man and woman, not young, shared the seat with two very small children.

Without quite knowing why, Reidel felt better. They were all dark-haired and dark-eyed, and their skin, like Reidel's own, was a color between bronze and pale brown. They wore loose coarse clothing, boys and girls alike dressed in faded blue trousers. They all stared shyly as the truck rattled into motion again; the old man spoke politely to Mathis and Mathis replied in a good imitation of his accent. Reidel, out of the conversation, listened and felt helpless.

Quite suddenly the truck rounded a curve and they were there. Mathis banged on the roof of the cab and the truck stopped; they got down, and to Reidel's surprise the man and woman inside got out, too.

Linnit was still lying in the inadequate shade of the thin trees. Reidel saw Arran furtively seize a weapon. Dionie ran toward them, crying out "Oh, you were gone so long—I hardly knew you in those clothes—"

Reidel shushed her imperatively. At such close distance, and in the presence not only of Mathis but of the telepathic Cleta, all the Dvanethy except Linnit—who was too weak and exhausted to raise her head, let alone listen—could clearly follow the conversation between Mathis and the man from the truck. He was saying "So your car burned, I see?"

Mathis, reading the other man's mental picture and translating the concepts into language, answered quietly, "Si. Ayer por la noche."

"Sua familia?"

The concept of a family was alien to Mathis, but he had been conditioned to an almost superhuman adaptability. He answered quickly in the affirmative as the man expected.

He knew what the man thought; that they were his own kind, Mexican migrant workers who had crossed the border, without legal permission, to work in the cotton fields. The Mexican had a very clear mental picture of Mathis' imagined predicament. And so adaptable were the telempaths that Mathis described it back to him graphically—the crash that had stranded himself and his large family here with a car that burned, a sick wife, a newborn child.

It did not really matter to Mathis or his listeners that he was picking the very words he used, like an invisible recording device, from his listeners' composite minds. He convinced them. By the time he finished he almost believed it himself. Also, because he was in close telepathic rapport with them all, by the time he finished he was speaking Mexican Spanish with an accent indistinguishable from that of the man, and at least Cleta and Dionie could speak easily in the new language.

The man offered, "Where we are going, they always need extra work hands, and they are not particular about residence cards. There is room for your family with us. Come with us; if the police find you here, they will send you back across the border." He added what Mathis already knew.

"My name is Vicente Arriagos."

His wife—they knew now she was his wife—came to Linnit, stooping to look into the tiny face folded into the sheet. "*Pobrecita*," she whispered, and picked up the baby in capable, motherly arms.

Cleta began to protest, but Dionie laid a restraining hand on her arm. She knew from a deep-down knowledge born of the empath's sensitivity to emotions that they were safe now.

In a short time Linnit had been lifted into the truck and a mattress pulled down, from the stacked household goods, for her to lie on. Room was made for all of them somehow, and the truck pulled away. Only Reidel looked back as they headed further and further from the place where the Dvanethy lifeship had crashed in the barren high plains of Texas

Space Bandit Search Wild Goose Chase

LUBBOCK, TEXAS: A search by highway patrolmen for two "space bandits" armed with what their victim described as "some sort of raygun" has ended in failure.

Edward Marcus, 23, told an incoherent story of having been held up on the borders of the huge Branzell ranch by two men dressed in "floating white robes like Arabs wear" after being accosted by a group of maybe "eight or ten" similarly dressed men and women who spoke halting English and claimed to have landed in a crashed "space-ship." They attacked Marcus with an unfamiliar weapon which rendered him helpless and incapable of motion. Marcus described it as "some kind of red gun with a shiny orange flame;" he told of listening helpless while the two men, whom he described as dark-skinned and dark-haired, searched his car and conversed in an unknown language. They stole only some spare clothes from a suitcase and about eighty dollars in cash.

Jerry Willett, Deputy Sheriff of Whiteface, Texas, discovered young Marcus unconscious in his automobile at the side of a private road into the million acre Branzell ranch. Willett drove him to a hospital in Lubbock, where he was treated for shock and exposure.

Sheriff Willett reported that the Marcus car showed no signs of a struggle, but that a suitcase containing ordinary clothing had been ransacked. Marcus' wallet, when found on the floor of the car, still contained over a hundred dollars in cash, and several credit cards which had not been touched. Routine investigation along the road located only a campsite probably used by transients.

Hospital personnel say they know of no weapon which could produce Marcus' symptoms of shock, partial paralysis and mild aphasia and amnesia. When asked if he were in a state of intoxication, they declined comment.

3

THE MAN who called himself Clint Landon put down his paper, scowled, and spoke one word,

"Dvanethy!"

Elizabeth Curran, at her desk across the room, raised her head. "What did you say, Mr. Landon?"

"Liz, did you read the paper—that space bandit story down in Texas?"

Liz chuckled. "They sell strong hooch down there."

"No, seriously. What did you think of it?"

Liz Curran's eyes grew grave. She was a tall young woman, not glamorous but remarkably pleasant-looking, with smooth dark hair and smiling eyes. "The ordinary flying saucer yarn, with a new twist," she remarked. "You'd think the sputniks and satallites would have killed most of that off, but they still turn up. Just the other day there was a saucer sighted in Texas—" She paused and frowned. "It was right around there, too. I knew the name rang a bell with me." She snapped her fingers and began to turn over some papers on her desk. "Darn! I knew I'd forgotten something, and that must have been it. I clipped it for your file." She located the clipping and handed it to Landon. "I'm sorry; I was making up that report on the Weber Electronics contract, the assemblyline thing, and forgot it. Yes, I thought so," she added. "It's the same name—Marcus. I'll bet he was drunk."

"You might lose," Landon said, not to the girl. He was studying the clippings, side by side, and Liz swung her chair around.

"Tell me something, will you, Mr. Landon? Seriously, now."

Landon laughed. "Fire away. I may not answer, but you can always ask."

Liz Curran looked at her employer for a minute without framing her question. On the surface there was nothing about him to mark him as different from any other businessman in the building, in the street, in the city; although, feature by feature, his face was striking, with strong proud bones and some indefinable dignity. He was a big man, not quite middle-aged, with dark hair just beginning to fade at the temples, and he looked like what he was: a competent, prosperous, professional man who had probably done hard manual work at some time.

Nothing mysterious—on the surface.

Finally she asked. "What do you get out of it, Mr. Landon, chasing down all these weird, flying saucer yarns? You're a perfectly respectable production-methods consultant, you've got more contracts than you can handle, but I'll bet—I'll bet a week's pay—that tomorrow you'll be on a plane to Texas, to check up on this space-bandit nonsense!"

"You lose," said Landon. "Not tomorrow, tonight." Then his face grew grave.

"Liz, you've heard about the man who cried 'Wolf'? There have been so many silly-season stories and hoaxes about flying saucers from outer space, that no one pays attention to them any more. If there should be a true story mixed in with the hallucinations and the cranks, it could easily get overlooked. Let's say—if it does, I want to know."

"I see," said Liz, grasping for a random memory. "The Branzell ranch—Branzell—I know that name."

"It's one of the biggest ranches in Texas," Landon said, "and he owns a newspaper. Retired now, but back when he was editing it himself, he—let me think. Yes, I checked one of his silly-season stories for him. Never met him, but he'd probably remember my name."

Liz regarded him, between a smile and a scowl.

"I smell a publicity stunt. And the Apperson Electronics contract is still hanging fire. You aren't going to chase off to Texas before that's signed, are you?"

Landon tapped his fingers indecisively on the desk. Finally he said "See if you can get Branzell for me on the phone, long distance. I'll talk to him first."

Liz nodded and picked up the phone.

This was no new occurrence to her. Landon was a freelance methods analyst, who worked in fields ranging from efficiency studies to factory-design layouts for assembly lines. He had an excellent reputation, commanded considerable fees, and between assignments turned out technical articles which were much in demand from the trade magazines.

But there was a Jekyll and Hyde angle to Landon the writer, as contrasted to Landon the businessman. Under a variety of pen names, he occasionally wrote highly colored science fiction; and during the last few years he had made a hobby of tracking down, and debunking, the so-called flying saucer stories.

Liz had Branzell on the phone.

"Hello, Steve? This is Clint Landon. You may not remember me, but I checked out the Canajoharie flying saucer scare for you, about four years back. Ring a bell?"

"I should say so," said the deep, positive voice at the far end of the wire. "You located the kids who built the thing out of scrap metal, and saved me a lot of trouble—not to mention saving my managing editor from making a darn fool of himself. Can I return the favor?"

"Could be. You've got yourself into the papers again, I see."

The pleasant voice was not quite so pleasant now.

"Clint, that sighting—it was straight. The Air Force people tracked it on radar, but they called it a meteor. Like I say, I thought it was a plane crash. We're near one of the Air Force training stations, and we thought a jet had come down. It's just—"

"I don't mean that," Landon interrupted. "I mean that space bandit thing."

Branzell swore so horribly that Liz, on the extension, was afraid they would cut him off the circuits. "The kid saw something, Clint. He's still in the hospital. Got a couple of funny burns."

Landon's face changed as if someone had hit him hard in the stomach.

"Burns? You said—burns? They couldn't be powder burns?"

"No, they're definitely not powder burns. The people at the hospital didn't pay much attention to them, but they looked at me like sulphur or magnesium burns. Damned queer."

"It is. Look, Steve, I wonder—"

"I know what you're going to say. I was just about to ask if you're still in the business of investigating these things."

"I'll be on the evening plane," said Landon grimly, "but let me warn you, Steve. If this is a publicity stunt, tip me off now. If you tell me it's on the level, and I find out that I've been had, I swear I'll tear up your Sunday edition and cram it down your gullet page by page!"

"If you're being had, then I'm being had too," Branzell said explosively, "and if you find out that one of my editors is making a fool of me, someone is going to get fired. I'll pay your expenses both ways—it's worth it to me, just to find out if it's a hoax."

"I'll see you this afternoon," said Landon, and hung up. Liz replaced her own extension and stared at her employer in dismay. "What about the Apperson contract?"

Landon looked troubled. "It can't be helped. Look, Liz—I know Branzell, and I don't think he'd pull a fast one. Someone might be hoaxing him, of course, but there's that one chance. Get me a flight on the noon plane. I'll go pack."

Lix Curran put her hands on her hips. Her dark eyes were spitting sparks.

"And you'll chase all the way off to Texas," she finally blurted, "just to expose a crackpot? Well, I hope you can debunk them high, wide and handsome!"

"Believe me," said Landon with heartfelt emphasis, "so do I."

She stared, open mouthed. "You—hope so?"

"Yes," Landon said harshly, "Just think, for a minute, about the alternatives."

He walked out, leaving her staring after him.

Landon climbed two flights of stairs to his apartment, where he dropped the calm professional manner like his hat and coat, and now he looked drawn and grim. He locked the door carefully, and put on a heavy night chain. An antique clock swung out on a pivot, exposing a thin sheet of glassy substance which could have been a mirror, but which reflected nothing but its own complex crystalline structure.

Including Mathis the telempath, riding in a jolting rattletrap across North Texas, exactly five people on the planet would have recognized the apparatus for what it was. Landon stood before it, in an attitude of fierce concentration, until a tiny pinpoint of light grew, deep down in the screen.

The man who received the message had not seen Landon in thirty years and would never see him again. Physically, he was somewhere in northern India. Translated, their conversation would have gone something like this if it had been in words.

—*Vialmir here.*

—*Clannon/Landon reporting. Some friends from home* (he weighted the words with all the telepathic symbolism they could carry) *may have landed in this hemisphere. I've just had an account of an attack with what sounds like a small shocker.*

—*There are no ships legally within the area in this timesector.*

—*Remember the meteor last night? I've got one spike on the photon-conversion tape. Just a tremor, a jiggle, but there's no normal photon-*

conversion on this planet. It would have been an implosion.

—*Which would mean an illegal landing; this planet is Closed.*

—*Yes, or it could be a crashed lifeship. In either case I'll have to investigate. Stand by—and wish me luck.*

—*You'll need it, Clannon.*

Clannon, or Landon, grinned bitterly. He swung the clock face shut and began packing.

Liz had been lucky about reservations. At three that afternoon Landon was in Lubbock, being shown past the cluttered editorial offices and thundering pressrooms to a quiet conference room. As he entered, a tall, immensely thin man, with a shock of unruly blonde hair still untouched by grey, rose and grasped his hand.

"Landon? Glad to know you."

Landon studied the man briefly as they sat down.

"I thought after that Canajoharie business you'd be sore, Steve. I spoiled a good story for your front page."

"The only good story is a true story," said Branzell, and the levelled, piercingly keen eyes met Landon's without flinching. "Let's get that much straight. If a story is a fake, I want to know it *before* it's printed, not after."

Landon nodded, satisfied. He could usually tell when he was being lied to. "Okay. Did the papers quote you accurately, then, or did they mix you up? You really saw it?"

"I saw a streak of fire, which could have been anything. Ned—young Marcus—went out and hunted, but hell, I've got a million acres and then some, all covered with mesquite and jackpine."

"And meteors burn up before they land, if it was a meteor. But this space-bandit business?"

Branzell leaned forward, fists clenched. "Landon, *something* happened to that kid. He wasn't drunk, either. I've never known him to drink more than a can of beer."

"He lives with you?"

"Not all the time," Branzell said. "This summer. Somebody got the idea there might be uranium deposits on the ranch, and I didn't feel like having a geological study made. But Ned, my nephew, was just out of engineering school, so I made him a proposition. He could go over the ground with a Geiger counter, look at the soil formations or whatever it is they do, and I'd give him a fat bonus if he found anything." He laughed deprecatingly. "Neither of us took it too seriously, I'm afraid."

"Was he badly hurt?"

"Dazed, mostly. He hardly seemed to know me when I came to the hospital."

That checked with what Landon knew of the shockers. He knew he would have to see the youngster in person; one look at the mysterious "burns" would prove or disprove his theory at a glance.

Branzell told him that Marcus had been discharged from the hospital that morning. "You'll come back to the ranch with me, of course. I'll lend you a car, and you can do your investigating from there."

When they were on the road, Landon said, "Steve, I hate to ask this. But—would the kid pull a hoax on you? Practical joke, maybe, not meaning any harm?"

Branzell kept his eyes on the road, answering slowly, "Offhand, I wouldn't think so," but Landon sensed he was being evasive.

"Look, Steve, no offense. There's something you're not telling me."

Branzell still did not look at him. His hands, gripped tight on the wheel, were shaking. "It sounds clean crazy."

Landon kept his voice neutral. "Whatever it is, Steve, I've heard crazier."

"Yeah," the older man said uneasily, swallowing, "You meet a lot of crackpots. Okay, take it or leave it. Sylvia, my niece, Sylvia predicted the damn meteor or whatever it was. Twenty minutes before it hit, she sent us out to watch for it. Next morning, she made Ned go out and hunt along that private road, the one where those—those people held him up."

Landon made no answer. He had none. Either Branzell was telling the truth, or he was an expert actor; in either case, Landon preferred to reserve judgment.

Branzell turned into a private road, pointed out the spot where the sheriff had found Marcus in his car, then drove a few more miles, pulled over to the side of the road, and stopped.

"This is where he found them. The sheriff says someone had camped here. I put up No TRESSPASS-ING signs, but they still—" Branzell suddenly flung the car door open and got out.

"What's going on in yonder? Hey you," he yelled, "can't you see this place is posted?"

There was a rustle, and a young man came out of the mesquite thicket. He was wearing levis and paratrooper boots, and a boxlike apparatus was strapped around his waist; Branzell's eyebrows went up when he saw it, and Landon tensed in apprehension; the thing was an expensive radiation counter.

"It's Marcus," Branzell said, adding to the youngster, "Good grief, Ned, I told you to take it easy for a day or so."

The kid didn't answer. He took a reeling step and then another, and suddenly Landon threw open the door on his side of the car and in one jump he ducked under the fence and reached the boy.

"He's sick, something's wrong," he said urgently. Branzell vaulted the fence and ran toward them.

"What's ailin' you, Ned?" he demanded.

Ned Marcus put his hands on the fence, leaning heavily across it. His face was a sick, dirty white. He gulped, swallowed hard, and managed to get the words out at last.

"Steve, I—I reckon you better get the sheriff back out here. There's a dead man back there in all that brushwood!"

4

LATE the next day, Landon met Liz Curran at the airport; and on the way back to the Branzell ranch he filled her in on the events that followed the discovery of the man's body.

Branzell had gone for the sheriff, leaving Landon and Marcus to stare suspiciously at one another for a long half-hour until he came back with the police. After a time the Rangers, arriving, had permitted them to approach and view the body, and Landon had gotten the shock of his life.

One look and his doubts had vanished.

He hadn't recognized the dead man himself, of course. But the strong racial stamp, not unlike his own, the faintly shimmering cloth in which the body was shrouded, the manner in which the dead face had been bound—this was no one born on Earth.

He had stood by, shaken and stiff, while they examined the body. "Mexican, I'd guess. Look, his chest's caved in."

"What will happen now?" Landon asked.

"The coroner will have to hold an inquest," the sheriff said callously, "Not a chance we'll ever identify him, though. Just one of those wetbacks. He'll wind up as John Doe, dead on arrival, and the county will get stuck for another funeral."

Landon felt oddly shaken as he looked down at the old man. Whether he was, as Landon felt, a scholar and a gentleman of a civilization beyond anything the sheriff could guess, or whether he was just what the others thought—an elderly pauper, cast out and abandoned—he had the dignity of age and death, and it moved Landon to impulsive protest.

"Bury him decently. I'll pay the expenses."

Branzell and Marcus had stared as if he were out of his mind. Then the police officer scowled too, and stared, and set his mouth.

He said, "I've chased out here three times in the last three days, and this time I damn near didn't come, because I thought it was more—" He used an unprintable word. "Look. This is no hit-and-run. Somebody stripped him to the skin, rolled him in a bedsheet—a damn good quality one— and hid him in the brush. Now, just as a matter of form, which of you ran over him? And why did you bother with that crazy space bandit yarn? This is manslaughter, and I'm going to get to the bottom of it."

As he drove through the clear sunlight, Liz' expectant profile tilted toward him, Landon wished he could confide in her. But he could only say, "Of course, it was very easy for me to prove I was in New York when the old man died. But Branzell didn't find it that easy." Troubled as he was, he smiled at the memory; Branzell wasn't used to accounting for his movements, and he hadn't liked it when they asked him to. Then he sobered.

"I like him, Liz. And he may be in real trouble."

"Then, you think what Marcus saw, may have been the real murderers?"

"I don't think there was any murder," Landon said, and lapsed into silence.

He felt overwhelmingly ill-equipped for his job. All the time he had been stationed on Earth, his duties had been almost nominal: to observe, and to make infrequent reports. The menace of the Rhu'inn was too acute, in this part of the Galaxy, to draw attention to any one planet by over-use of communications. Thousand-to-one contingencies like this one were not provided for in his instructions. He could act at discretion, provided he did not imperil his secrecy, or neglect his primary reason for being on Earth.

"Liz," he said, "I want you to go through every paper published in Texas. City dailies, small-town weeklies. Comb through them for anything unusual—anything at all out of the way."

"Flying saucers?"

"Or anything else."

"And what will you be doing, then?"

"I'd be only too glad to tell you, if I knew, Liz," Landon said and lapsed into grim silence again.

Because, if I could tell you, it would mean I knew what I'd be doing.

But he knew just one shattering fact. A lifeship from the Dvaneth Federation had landed and imploded. There had been survivors and one casualty. But where had they gone? What could they do?

There was only one thing they could do; submerge themselves in the planet, let the ripples close noiselessly over their heads, as he himself had done. The longer he delayed in finding them, the less likely it became that he ever would. It would become harder and harder to distinguish them from Earthmen, as they adapted to this world.

But just at first they might make some mistake, and he might find them by it.

He left Liz, and drove to a large electrical-supply house. Then he thought better of it and drove on to a large mail-order firm where he bought a pocket-size Geiger-Muller "snooper" model radiation counter. It wasn't a particularly sensitive instrument. But it would register what he was looking for—if it was there to be registered.

He drove alone along the road to the ranch, parked the car, slipped through the fence, and located the marks of the fire. Yes, someone had camped here. He went over the ground almost inch by inch, and before long his search was rewarded by a torn scrap of something too thick to be paper, too thin to be plastic. Landon flexed it between his fingers. There was a whirring sound, and a voice spoke several Dvaneth syllables. Obviously this bit of the recording wrapper had escaped the destruction imposed by Dvaneth law for all artifacts on non-Federation planets, or else the mysterious survivors had ignored the law. Landon put it in his pocket to be burnt, glad the sheriff had not found it.

He searched, but found nothing further. The Geiger was clucking softly to itself at background level, but no more, and Landon felt frustrated. The site of the implosion couldn't be too far away. The man with the crushed chest, for instance, couldn't have gotten very far.

The residual radiation might still guide him to the implosion site, if he was lucky. He could hardly cover eight or ten square miles of mesquite grassland on foot. What he really needed was a high-grade scintillation counter, but that was nothing anyone could carry in a pocket.

A noise in the underbrush made him stop and thrust the Geiger inside his coat. Out of the mesquite walked Ned Marcus.

"Well, this is a surprise," Marcus said. But he didn't sound precisely pleased.

"Hunting up your space bandits?"

"The police let me go when the hospital verified my story. I came back to see what I could find here. They've got Steve Branzell in jail. Or didn't you know?"

"I know. I think we're looking for the same thing," Landon said rather grimly. He had just realized that he could not read Ned Marcus' mind.

Landon was not a good natural telepath. However, like all Dvanethy, he had had some training; with some effort he could usually read an unwary mind.

But Ned Marcus, like many men on this overpopulated, city-plugged planet, had developed excellent defenses against unconscious brainpicking by passers-by. People who did not officially recognize the existence of telepathy often had, Landon had found, the best natural defenses against it. And rare individuals like Marcus had a perfect natural barrier.

Landon called it shuttlethinking—shifting the mind quickly back and forth among several related topics, so that an ordinary telepath, probing without special equipment, could not follow any single one without revealing himself. Not ready to reveal himself, Landon abandoned the effort.

Marcus had his scintillation counter slung over his shoulder. It was an expensive one, equipped with delicate external probes and a special subsurface probing device. It was exactly the kind of instrument Landon had wanted, but hadn't wanted to take a chance on renting or buying; equipment houses usually kept close track of the sale of such delicate, expensive machinery, and ostensibly Landon had no real excuse for owning one.

"You don't believe in flying saucers, do you?" Marcus demanded belligerently.

"I believe what I see," Landon evaded.

"And you think, if you look around long enough, you'll see one here?"

"Let's quit kidding around," Landon said. "I came out here for the same thing you did, I imagine—to see what I could find to back up your space bandit story, or figure out if you stumbled across an ordinary murder, or what. So let's hunt for it together."

"I'll buy that, for the moment," Marcus said. "My car's parked up there, and I've got some beer in a cooler. Let's walk back and have some."

Landon followed. He was very conscious of the muffled clicking of his small Geiger counter. Even silenced by the folds of his coat, it sounded like a rather noisy cricket. But Marcus seemed not to notice. They found his parked car, and Marcus reached into the seat, to lift out a portable cooler, while Landon strolled away to look across the large expanse of land visible from the knoll.

Click. Click. Click-click-click—

The sudden swiftening of the hidden gadget sounded like a kettledrum to Landon, but Marcus did not seem to hear; he rummaged in the dashboard compartment, found an opener, punched a hole in the beercan and handed it, dripping white foam, to Landon. He punched another for himself.

"Thanks." Landon lifted the can and drank, but Marcus tipped his head, listening.

Click-click-click-clickety

"What the hell—" Landon staggered from the impact as the can was knocked from his hand; with a violent jerk, Marcus thrust a hand into his coat pocket and ripped out the Geiger. "I thought so!" He dashed the thing to the ground, where it lay chuckling to itself. "Wise guy!"

"I can explain—"

"You're good at explaining!" Marcus glared at him. "The trouble is, believing it! Are you from one of the big mining or processing companies? That's the only thing that makes sense. You're trying to buy up mineral rights before Branzell finds out what a lease is worth! And you rigged this saucer nonsense to scare off sound investors!"

Landon laughed.

"If you'll look at that thing, you'll see I couldn't be doing any serious prospecting with it. It's just a toy." He bent to retrieve it, but Marcus, with a vicious thrust of his leg, kicked it out of reach. It stopped muttering.

Landon looked warily at the youngster, wondering if he were going to have to fight. "It sounds as if you'd made a find, and you're afraid I'll try to cash in on it. Let's get things straight. You're working for Branzell, I'm not. You'd get paid if anything turned up here, not me. But there isn't a gram of uranium around here."

Marcus only glowered. "You'd like me to believe that, wouldn't you? I'm wondering if the FBI wouldn't be interested."

Landon thought faster than he had ever thought in all his years on earth. He *had* to prevent a scientific study of this area. A college kid with a radiation counter was one thing; a team of professionals combing the area was something else. Marcus was advancing on him, menacingly.

"I don't know just what you're up to, Landon, but I sure as hell don't like it. Flying saucers—holy jumping Moses!"

Landon began to feel he'd even underestimated the kid. Physically he wasn't a match for Marcus, if it came to a fight, and anyway he couldn't risk trouble. His whole carefully-built identity of Clint Landon had been based on the assumption that as long as a man minds his own business, pays his taxes, and avoids the company of criminals and the vicinity of crime, he can get away with almost any kind of secret aims and pursuits. But his background would not stand detailed investigation, and the slightest glimmer of publicity would be disastrous now.

The dead man wasn't conclusive proof that the survivors were harmless marooned Dvanethy. Rhu'inn could have made this use of an unlucky captive or casualty—they used their human victims ruthlessly—to throw a Watcher off the trail. At whatever cost, he had to keep his freedom of movement. And that meant taking the most desperate chance of all.

"I know what you found," he said. "That blackish patch over there."

Marcus half-turned his head, regarding Landon with sullen distrust. "I saw it."

"Did you try a subsurface probe? You know my little tick-tock won't pick up anything like that. I can tell you exactly what you'll find."

"Because you planted it there yourself?"

Landon said wearily, "I haven't been in Texas

since before they invented Geiger counters and I can prove it.'' Marcus hesitated and Landon pressed his advantage. "I know what made it. You'll find a small, circular patch of charred grass, ringed with radioactive carbon. Inside the patch you'll find a few ounces of heavy, reddish dust. It will make your scintillator go wild, but you can handle it with fair safety for about five minutes; then it will start to blister your fingers. It won't scatter in the wind; it's superheavy. And if you took it to experts," he paused, "—you'd be told it didn't exist and this whole area would be put under military guard.''

"I don't understand—''

"And I won't explain now, because you wouldn't believe me." Landon was weighing his chances. If this failed, he might have to kill Marcus and disappear. Weighing one life against the millions who would suffer if the Rhu'inn got loose on a planet this size, Marcus didn't matter, and neither did he, Landon. But he didn't want too many. "My counter won't work. You saw to that. By the way, you owe me thirty bucks. So you find it.''

Marcus glared down at him and Landon would have given ten years of his life to get past that shuttlethinking outer guard. Finally the kid swung the scintillator over his shoulder.

"You win. But when I find it—*if* I find it—you'd better have a story I can believe, or I'll have the FBI here inside an hour.''

5

THE SUN blinded Reidel moving slowly down the row, dragging the heavy cottonsack, stripping each plant with automatic motions.

He was darker, burned by the unfamiliar sun. The work, though arduous, did not bother him. The process of adaptation had done its swiftest work on Reidel; not unintelligent, he was almost without imagination. He reserved problems of tomorrow for tomorrow's settlement, and welcomed the physical rigor of the work, which left him no time for thoughts, regrets or hopes better put aside.

The sun was nearly down. One by one, the pickers in the field came up the long rows, and Reidel went to help Mathis weigh the heavy sacks. At first he had been upset when the owner, Foster—who hadn't given them more than the barest glance, when they turned up with Vincente—singled out Mathis as weigher-checker. But it made sense—a task physically lighter, yet demanding trustworthiness and intelligence.

Reidel knew that Mathis, with his insinuating telempathic abilities, was building up that impression of his own trustworthiness. Under this onslaught it was natural that Foster should have offered the post, and it would certainly have made Mathis more conspicuous to refuse than to accept.

Dionie came toward the truck, and Reidel frowned, worried. Her face looked flushed again. She had been very sick after her first day in the fields, with fever, and her skin was still peeling off in flakes. Reidel, of course, had never seen acute sunburn, and did not know what it was.

Cleta, last in the line of pickers, gave up a sack much too heavy for her. She drew off the rough cotton gloves worn by all pickers, folded them daintily and put them in the pocket of the coarse, faded man's jacket she was wearing. Her delicate fingers were roughened, the beautiful complexion darkened by fierce sun and wind, and her spun-silk hair bleached into brownish streaks, but she stood there with the same aloof dignity as if she were at a planetary council ball. Reidel went to her and said, "Cleta, you're overdoing. Tomorrow you had better stay and look after Linnit."

Her dark grave eyes stared past him. "Linnit doesn't need me, and I don't need pampering. Mind your own business, Reidel."

He spun around and walked away. He could have choked her. If she had ever shirked or complained, he could have borne it.

Foster drove away, the cotton trailer bumping and swaying, and the pickers who lived in the barracks climbed up into Vincente's rattletrap truck.

The two bare barrack rooms allotted to them, now seemed home and familiar, despite their squalor—the rickety beds covered with faded worn blankets, the battered furniture from the junk shop. Linnit's baby, in a dirty diaper, lay gurgling to herself in a splintery basket lined with a soft pink blanket which was the only new thing in the place. Linnit, her dark stringy braids accentuating the pallor of her bony face, smiled as she put chipped dishes on the table. There was a warm, intriguing smell of hot food.

Reidel, sleeves rolled back, went to the faucet to wash. He fumbled, dripping, for a towel Cleta had taken, turned and saw her standing there, as remote as if she were on another planet. She had taken off the faded sacklike dress and stood there in a clean cotton petticoat and nothing else, completely and coldly unaware of his presence.

Reidel had grown used to the lack of privacy here; Linnit and Dionie were little more than children, and never distrubed him in the slightest. But now, jabbed in a raw place, he snarled at her, "Get some clothes on, you—" He flung a word at her from the gutters of the spaceports. The girl could have understood nothing but its foulness, but no one with a scrap of telepathy could possibly have mistaken his meaning. She went white. Then, as if seeing Reidel for the first time, she stood frozen, her head thrown back, something coming alive in her eyes that had never stirred there before.

Then, gasping, she snatched at the damp towel, hugging it convulsively to her bare breast, and fled into the other room.

Slowly, Reidel let out his breath. He could not help wondering. Was this an echo of the conditioning none of them would ever remember? This urge, this biological awareness, out of all sensible context of time and place? He disliked Cleta; the emotion she roused in him, for no good reason, drove him to baffled rage. Urge for survival or no urge for survival, it was a damned nuisance. Oh, yes, Cleta was a pretty woman. She was a desirable one. But he'd be *damned* if he was going to be shoved around by some conditioned reflex or other!

He went into the other room and sat down. "Where's Arran?"

Cleta twisted her pretty mouth. "You think you have to watch us all, every minute, don't you?"

Reidel's chair slammed backward. A shrill wail came from the basket, and Linnit reached for her child, saying plaintively, "She was just going to sleep!"

Reidel set the chair on its legs with exaggerated quiet, but the door banged on protesting hinges behind him.

It was dark now, but Reidel could make out the familiar outline of a young man's back, silhouetted against a half-open door, merging into another silhouette; full cotton skirts and long curls slipped away into darkness as Reidel's foot scrunched gravel. The crack of light slid shut.

"Arran?"

The boy whirled, his words choking with rage. "Just stay out of my life, will you?"

"Arran, be reasonable. You're apt to get more deeply involved than you realize, meddling with their women," Reidel warned. "Mathis told us about the social taboos here—"

Arran's mouth was tight and ugly. "You grudge me the slightest, but you and Cleta—"

"You fool, she treats me like a piece of furniture." Suddenly Reidel realized that he was shaking with the suppressed impulse to smash his fist into Arran's face, explode in violence. He shouted, "I hate the damned girl!"

When they got back, the others had finished their meal. The food was cold, a stiffening mess, but Reidel ate without tasting. Dionie drew a jacket around her shoulders. "I'm going to the store for tomorrow," she said. Reidel asked "Have you enough money?" and handed her a bill from his jacket pocket, musing briefly on the pattern of relationships that had grown up between the members of the group.

Family feelings, as such, were alien to the Dvanethy, and he wondered if this were a pattern of their adaptation. Dionie went out, and Cleta put the baby in Linnit's lap and gathered up the dirty dishes. Arran, rising to help, said with a sour smile, "We're certainly getting adapted!"

Cleta almost dropped a plate at his tone, but Arran went on a minor explosion, "Slavery and filth! What a planet we picked!"

"We didn't have much choice," Cleta said coolly, "and we won't be here forever."

Arran, his face suffused with color, was about to answer, but a knock at the door cut off his words, and Reidel opened it to see Nick Foster standing there.

He said, through his surprise, "Won't you come in?"

Foster's face stiffened; Reidel saw it and was annoyed in turn. "No," Foster said curtly, "thanks. Is there a girl here named Cleta?"

"What do you want with her?"

Foster, no fool, heard the suspicion in Arran's tone. "Nothing. My wife asked me to find a girl to help in the house. She looks clean and handy, and we'll pay her more than she could make in the field."

Reidel wished he were a telepath; a beautiful girl is a saleable commodity on any planet, and he didn't suppose this one was any exception. He hesitated until Cleta came out, wiping soapsuds away with a towel.

Mathis said curtly, "Let her go, Reidel, if she wants to," and when Foster was out of earshot the telempath said with contempt, "Foster is not a good man, but he does not care much for women, even his own. Cleta will have to work hard, but she will not be in the sun all day. And we might as well see something of the way others live in this world."

"I only thought we should stay together," Reidel demurred, but Cleta pushed past him angrily. "I didn't ask you," she said, and began to rattle dishes violently together.

Suddenly, shrilly, a scream ripped through the barracks, a high shriek of terror. Cleta dropped a cup with a crash. Mathis, suddenly convulsed, thrust out his hands in a spasm of rejection. "No, no," he said hoarsely, "*Dionie*" and crumpled. Arran caught his senseless body, but Reidel was already out the door.

Arran let Mathis slide, inert, to the floor and ran, Cleta at his heels. The night was full of footsteps and noises and confused questions from the barracks doors, but Cleta ran unerringly toward a small narrow alleyway leading to a row of deserted buildings. As Reidel turned this way and that, Dionie shrieked again and someone thrust past him, knocking him almost off his feet, and disappeared into darkness.

In the alley, Dionie was lying on the ground, her flimsy blouse ripped to the waist. Reidel brushed Cleta aside and lifted the sobbing child into his arms. His face was bleak and grim as he carried her back toward their rooms, her face pressed into his shirt, shielding her from the curious faces that had popped out of all the doors. Arran, panting with exertion, raced back along the gravel.

"I nearly had the—the unspeakable creature in my hands," he said between shaken gasps, "but he got loose, lucky for him—I'd have killed him!"

Cleta laid her hand on Reidel's arm. "Reidel," she whispered, "Dionie's not hurt, only frightened. He ran away when she screamed."

Linnit, kneeling by Mathis, looked up in dismay as Reidel carried Dionie into the room. Cleta came to take Dionie in her arms, and over the tousled head her eyes met Reidel's with implacable hatred. "This damnable place! Why did you bring us here?"

Reidel could not answer. Now that he knew Dionie was not seriously hurt, his rage was giving way to shaking bewilderment. What insane, incredible sort of world was it, where a girl Dionie's age was not safe? And the freak coloring of a hypersensitive empath would have protected her in the stewing hells of a Capella slum!

Mathis was still trembling with the traumatic shock of the experience. Doubtless he had felt all Dionie's terror. Arran was watching with a grim, inscrutable look. Between diminishing sobs, Dionie whispered, "He didn't really do anything but tear my dress, but I—I felt everything he—he—oh, it was horrible, horrible!" She shuddered, hiding her face again.

They had all drawn close; Reidel still holding Dionie, Cleta kneeling at his side, arms around the girl; Arran and Linnit watching anxiously and even Mathis, who usually held himself rigidly apart, rejecting the pull of their emotions, laying a shaking hand on Dionie's shoulder.

Reidel literally did not trust himself to look up. Cleta's eyes were like a magnet; he seemed to feel them through the top of his bent head. Something was coming alive in him that had been dormant, numbed by shock and the unfamiliar surroundings, until this moment of close rapport between them had brought it to life again. He looked at the room with new and hating eyes. Suddenly he was edgily frantic lest the telepathic Cleta should sense this, as she had sensed Dionie's peril and her safety.

Cleta laid a hand on his arm again. "Reidel, listen to me," she said, but it broke the last threat of his control. With sudden, agonized violence he rose to his feet, thrusting Dionie away from him, spun on his heel and slammed out of the room.

6

"But what the devil is it?" Ned Marcus sat back on his heels, skepticism gone downwind as he touched, with a cautious fingertip, the strange dark-red dust.

"We call the process implosion, which is a layman's term and not accurate," said Landon slowly. "It's a form of molecular disintegration. Matter itself can't be destroyed, of course, but implosion destroys the atomic orientation of the particles. The space lattice collapses, and each element breaks down into free hydrogen, free neutrons and radiocarbon. All, that is, except this red dust, which is an allomorphic precipitate of the radioactive bromine compounds used in the fuel."

"Fuel for what? Your flying saucers?"

"No. Scoop up that dust in a beer can, or something, before someone else gets smart with a radiation counter. I might as well explain to all of you at once. There's no sense in going over it again and again."

As they turned into the driveway before the Branzell ranch house, Landon noticed the station wagon with the BR monogram of the Branzell Ranch on the doors, parked in the drive. "Branzell's back, so I can tell him, too. Find a fruit jar or something—glass or enamel—and stow that bromine residue, will you? It isn't safe in metal for very long."

Steve Branzell was in the big, shaded living room with Liz, who stood up quickly as they came in. Landon faced Branzell a little wearily.

"I found what I was looking for, Steve. I apologize for ever thinking it might be a hoax."

Branzell's sharp blue eyes looked guarded, and not too well pleased. "If I were fixing up a hoax, I'd hardly arrange to get myself booked on suspicion of manslaughter," he said dryly. "That's carrying a publicity stunt too far. My lawyers got me out. It seems they didn't even have enough to book me." He turned away, and Landon saw that there was another woman in the room, or rather, another girl—a slim, fair-haired girl with a childish face and wide blue eyes.

Marcus, following Landon's glance, said briefly, "My sister Sylvia, Mr. Landon." He gave the blonde girl a hard-eyed stare. "No, sis, cut it out."

Landon began, "This is the one—?" But he broke off, for Sylvia was regarding him with a peculiar, fixed stare. Branzell asked, "Shall I have the staff get some drinks?" Landon motioned him to silence, sensing the tentative touch. In amazement he realized Sylvia Marcus was a telepath, and an exceptionally sensitive one. And Landon, never expecting this had not thought to barricade himself. The girl stared at him stark white, and ran a small pink tongue over her lips.

"My parents should have named me Cassandra," she said weakly. "Who'd believe it?" She turned and almost ran from the room.

Liz said flippantly, "She doesn't seem to have liked what you were thinking. Mr. Landon," But Landon only sat staring numbly at the door through which Sylvia had vanished, wondering what he had given away. He was more baffled than ever. How could a telepath of Sylvia's sensitivity live in the same family with a shuttlethinker like Marcus and stay sane? And Branzell was aware of her powers.

Marcus broke in with a belligerent, "Well, how about those explanations?" and set the radio-bromine on the table. Landon sighed and said, "I'll start from the beginning. It's a long story."

An hour later, he faced them and finished. "That's really all there is to tell. After that, I just drifted to where I am now. Worked in a machine shop, went to engineering school, got into methods analysis. The writing began as an exercise in the language, and it let me investigate queer things without attracting too much attention.

Sylvia had slipped back into the room and was regarding him with interest. She was the only one who had not had even a fleeting doubt. Branzell was frowning.

"Clint, I've heard a lot of fantastic yarns, but this tops them all. If anyone else told me that story, I'd throw him out on his pratt."

"There's no doubt about it," Sylvia said somberly. Her hand rested on Branzell's shoulder, and Landon was aware of the close rapport between them and of the exact moment when Branzell's doubts began to crumble, and why.

Doubtless, once Branzell had been a telepath himself, more sensitive by far than Landon. And he must have been derided for it; meeting endless charlatans and phonies, in his search to understand; coming up against those who simulated the real thing by lying tricks. Branzell had developed a perfect defense—cynical belief that his own telepathic sensitivity was a pleasant hallucination, a form of wishful thinking. Yet he believed Sylvia, and the confusion was painful.

Sylvia looked up into Landon's eyes and said quietly, "Don't judge either of us harshly, Clannon. This world is hard on the different ones, and there is no understanding. Only fear."

"It explains a lot about you," said Liz uneasily, "but—you're really human?"

On that point he could be instantly reassuring. "Good lord, yes! Did you think I was a monster crawled inside a human skin?"

Marcus asked dryly, "How would we know the difference?"

The question made Landon shiver. He was human, yes all the way through. But one race in the Galaxy could do exactly that—the Rhu'inn, the protean, tenuous horror of a million worlds. He had told them everything else, but of this, Landon would not speak—the horror that could crawl inside a man and use him against his own kind.

He pretended to misunderstand the question. "The subrace I belong to would fit in a little better in Peru or Mexico, but I picked North America because I liked the opportunities for technical education."

"That's flattering," said Branzell dryly.

Liz asked, "What are the flying saucers really?"

"I haven't the faintest idea. But the persistent reports of them are one reason I'm stationed here."

Marcus came back to the immediate problem. "And you suspect a ship from outside has landed here?"

"I don't suspect it, I know it. There's nothing in the universe which remotely resembles the implosion residue of radiobromine fuel."

"But why do you want to risk discovery yourself, to hunt up these people?" Marcus demanded.

Liz stared at Marcus. "Why, he has to find them! Think how frightened and lost they must feel!"

Marcus muttered, "The two I met didn't seem very frightened, or very lost."

Landon wished he could get a glimpse inside that shuttlethinking. "I'm empowered to make your losses good. We respect property rights absolutely in the Dvaneth Federation, but the condition known as 'desperate need involving the alternative of loss of life or starvation' creates a primary right to an obvious surplus, even in law. You notice they didn't take all your clothes or your money."

"Sounds hair-splitting," Branzell murmured, "and a trifle Utopian."

"What I want to know is this," Marcus broke in rudely, "how did they happen to speak English?"

"There must have been a telempath with them," Landon said, then was struck by a sudden incongruity. If they had read Marcus' mind, how was it that he, Landon, could not? Was it possible that Marcus could turn that shuttlethinking on, and off, at will? That would be something new.

"And what happens when you find them?" Branzell wanted to know. "Can you signal your home world that you've picked up some strays?"

Landon shook his head, explaining. Dvanethy

marooned on Closed Planets had to be abandoned. Rescue work, dangerous and expensive anywhere, was an impossible risk on a Closed Planet.

He hoped Sylvia would not try to read his mind. Try as he might, he could not prevent the ominous thought of the Rhu'inn from sneaking into the far corners of his brain. Probably they were harmless survivors of a wrecked trading or colony ship. There was an off chance that it was an illegal entry; but anyone daring the extreme penalty of Federation law by landing on a Closed Planet, any fugitives hiding from Dvanethy justice on a world where they knew no outsider could follow, would have known enough to scatter or hide the implosion residue that would be sure to give them away to the planet's Watcher.

He stood up. "Marcus, I want the best description you can give me of them. They'll adapt, yes, but I'd like to find them first. And it won't be easy for them. It wasn't easy for me, and I came here in the days when a man could still get along without a birth certificate and a draft card."

Branzell began to pace the floor. "What absolutely rotten luck," he said vehemently. "They land right on my ranch, and then they vanish into thin air again. Where could they have gone? Damn it, Clint, where could they go?" He swung round. "There's no one around here at all, except my ranch hands, and a few Mexican workers on the cotton farms in the Brazos valley—"

He stopped; Liz and Sylvia stared, openmouthed. "And you look like a Mexican, Landon. That didn't take any mind-reading."

Landon slumped. "But how many Mexican labor camps are there? And would anyone take them on? Don't they have to be vouched for by the Mexican government, or something?"

The rancher nodded. "Yes, before you can hire braceros you're supposed to get a work card for every man, woman and kid on your place," he admitted. "Of course, some of them do come into the country illegally. I can pull a few strings, maybe, and find out which of the ranchers around here aren't too particular about immigration permits. Meanwhile, Landon, you're welcome to use the ranch, or the newspaper offices, for your base of operations. Maybe the staff could help Miss Curran with her newspaper search for unusual events—"

Landon instantly vetoed that; the fewer who knew about it, the better. Branzell yielded the point, but sighed.

"I'd like to put the whole staff to work on it. Clint, all I ask is this. If you ever do make it public, give me the first chance at an interview, will you? And whether we can print it or not, when you find them, I want to talk to them!"

That much Landon could promise with a clear conscience.

7

NOT FAR from the barracks, near the railroad siding where the cotton was loaded and shipped, there were stock pens, and the evening freight train often stopped to load or unload cattle, calves and sheep.

Reidel had taken to leaving the barracks each evening, and strolling across to watch the animals and the skill, or lack of it, with which they were handled. One evening Cleta detained him with a quiet, "Reidel, wait—"

He made no answer except an ungracious noise. Since the evening he had walked out on her, he had tried to avoid her. This was made easier by the fact that she no longer came into the fields. Now, for the first time, he became aware of an astonishing change in her. Her roughened hands still bore the marks of hard work, but they looked well-tended; her hair had been combed into smooth ringlets and she had done something to her coarse, faded clothes to make them look neat and feminine. He suddenly lost his anxiety to be away from her.

"Where do you go every night, Reidel?"

"Out to watch the stock pens."

She said in apology, "We haven't made it too easy for you, have we? You and I seem to spend most of our time fighting and then apologizing, don't we?"

"I can think of worse ways to spend my time."
Reidel felt astonishingly lighthearted. "Let's fight
some more."

Cleta giggled and he added, "Or—why not
come with me and watch?"

She hesitated just long enough for his bitterness
to surge back. "Or don't you care to be seen with a
roughneck like me?"

"Of course I'll come!" she said warmly. "I just
meant to tell you. Mrs. Foster mentioned that Foster had a prize bull coming in on the train tonight.
You're interested in things like that, aren't you?"

Reidel was touched that she would remember
and mention this.

Cleta flushed. "Working at the Foster house and
seeing how some people live here—it makes me
want to fight this!" She gestured around her.
"Dionie's getting to look like these grubby children, running about barefoot. Linnit sits there
with those cows of women, the baby kicking in
the dirt, perfectly happy. That's what's so awful,
Reidel, they're happy."

Reidel turned and laid his hands on her shoulders.

"Do you really hate to see anyone happy?"

"No, no, I'm not as cruel as that, it's only—oh,
Reidel, it's getting at me too, it's like an invisible
tide sucking me under—"

"Cleta, girl!" His hands tightened and she let
herself fall against him, sobbing desolately.

He waited till she quieted a little. Then he said
softly, "You'll have to be patient. Why do you
think I come here? The same reason, I think, that
you watch Foster's wife and daughter—and it's
already changed you."

"Cleta—" Reidel drew her back into the

shadows, so that they were shielded from sight by a corner of the fence. He hardly knew what he meant to say, until he spoke her name; and then he didn't say it. He only pulled her close again and kissed her with hungry, helpless violence.

She was startled and passive for a moment, then her arms went around him. "That won't solve anything," she said, but her voice was softer than he had ever heard it.

With an intensity that blurred rational judgement from his voice Reidel said, "Cleta, I'm—I'm frightened for you. I want to take care of you. I don't even know what it is I want. Not just the mating privilege we'd give or grant on Dvaneth. I want the right to—" he fumbled with unfamiliar words, even unfamiliar thoughts, "to keep you from working too hard. To make you a little less unhappy. I wish it could be—our own way, Cleta. But —will you marry me?"

She laced his fingers through hers, but she did not look up at him. "I couldn't—not the way it would have to be here, one man and one woman, and a permanent commitment that might last all our lives. I simply haven't adapted that far. And suppose we had children? I'd be like Linnit— afraid for them, but not caring about anything else."

"But Linnit's happy," Reidel reminded her very softly.

A blaze of electric light illuminated the stock pens and Reidel, blinking in the glare, saw that Cleta's eyes were wet.

"The train must be coming, I hear the whistle and there's Mathis."

"What are you doing here?" Reidel demanded as Mathis approached. "Is anything wrong?"

"Everything's fine. I only wanted to see what was the mysterious fascination of this place—to lure away not only you, but Cleta?"

They paid no attention; Reidel because he had trained himself to ignore the dwarf's sarcasm, and Cleta because, telepathic, she knew there was no real malice behind it. They made room for him beside them as the train shuffled to a halt.

A man from the local newspaper had come with a camera and was snapping flashbulbs toward the prize bull. Foster and two of his foremen were edging around carefully, trying to get close to the animal; Reidel moved along the fence to where he could watch without getting in the way.

The bull snorted and heaved up his head, pawing at the straw. Reidel studied it with an expert's eye. *Good breeding stock, but vicious; he'd have had it gelded as a calf.* His contempt for Foster increased as he saw the ineffectual way the man was bossing the unloading. If he could have followed his inclinations, Reidel would have shoved them all aside and said, "Here, you idiots, let me do that."

Mathis frowned and muttered, "Foster's getting angry. Doesn't he know the bull will smell it on him?"

"It will charge him—" Reidel gripped the fence. And then it happened; the bull lunged, crashed through the wooden rails nailed across the boxcar door, and hurled a ton of power straight at Foster. The men leaped up on the fence. The bull crashed into the rails, and the impact hurled Foster to the ground inside the pen.

Reidel was over the fence in one leap. He ran only a few steps, but they seemed endless. On Dvaneth he had twice won a green banner for his sport. *Skills deteriorate if you don't use them,* he thought frantically. *Can I still do it?*

Then he was hurtling at the bull's body and in another instant had stopped its charge and vaulted clear. The bull, stopped in mid-lunge, but only briefly, saw a new tormentor; he turned from Foster and the foreman dragged the dazed man safely outside the fence while Reidel, getting one arm around the bull's neck, braced his foot in the flank and clung there, swaying with the animal's maddened plunges, sending a wordless scream to Mathis. The bull tossed his head and plunged, trying to fling this leech into the dirt and stamp on him.

Then the bull stopped, planting his feet, and Reidel let himself slide, trembling, to the ground. Mathis hobbled close and patted the heaving neck, and Reidel, breathing hard, leaned against the animal's sweating sides. Mathis had certainly saved both their lives. It was easy to grab a bull if you knew the trick of it, but if Mathis hadn't thrown himself into the empathic rapport, he'd have been thrown off sooner or later and trampled. Only a telempath could handle a really maddened animal, and Reidel had never seen a meaner one.

Foster, limping on an ankle twisted in his fall, stopped a wary few steps away, and stared.

"Man, you ought to be in the rodeo! I sure thought I'd had it! Hey, don't you two live in my barracks? What are you—a bullfighter?"

Reidel shook his head, still panting with effort, hardly noticing the flashbulb that snapped bright in his eyes. "No, but I'm trained to handle them. Mathis hypnotized him so you won't have any trouble now for a few hours, but you need an empath to handle a vicious beast like this."

"Hypnotized?" Foster snorted laughter. "I guess he did, at that. The critter seems all right now." His hand went to his pocket, but Reidel made a gesture of proud rejection.

"Keep your money!"

Foster, seeing anger blazing in the dark eyes, swiftly returned the money to his wallet. "No offense meant, but a man who can handle a bull like that is wasted pulling cotton. Reidel, come to the office tomorrow and maybe I can find you something better to do."

"Now you've really done it!" Mathis' voice was acid, searing Reidel's tired brain. Reidel said wearily, "What else could I have done? Could I let a man be trampled and savaged before my eyes?"

"Did you have to babble all that about hypnotism and empaths?" Mathis snarled. Reidel felt Cleta's gentle touch on his arm. "Of course you had to do what you did," she said. "But now there's no help for it; we'll have to go away."

Reidel walked a few steps without answering. He was weary and shaking with exertion, but he felt more like his old self than ever.

"All right," he said at last. "We'll go whenever you say."

Prominent Rancher Escapes Death From Savage Champion Bull

Bracero Plays Toreador!

CLEARWATER, TEXAS: Nicholas Foster, cotton rancher and owner of one of Texas' finest herds of dairy cattle, narrowly escaped death yesterday under the hoofs of Westwoods Champion III, prize Guernsey bull valued at $30,000. The bull was being unloaded at the Clearwater siding when he went berserk and charged. Tragedy was averted when two Mexican nationals employed by Foster jumped into the pen and diverted the bull's attention.

Pictured above are the two men, identified by Foster as Roy Reydel and Mathis Reydel. The younger man seized the bull's horns and bulldogged him, rodeo style, while the older man supposedly subdued the animal by gazing into his eyes and hypnotizing him.

8

"CLINT, I wish you'd look at this." Liz Curran handed him the clipping. "Didn't Marcus say—"

Ned Marcus came up behind them and bent over Liz' shoulder. He took the clipping without asking leave, read it through, and frowned at the picture. "It could be the one," he said, "the hunchback. The other man—there's nothing unusual about him except the way he's dressed. In a shirt and pants he'd look like anybody."

Clint Landon read the clipping through again and scowled. "That bull hypnotizing trick doesn't sound like ordinary rodeo. I wouldn't spell the Dvaneth Reidel as Reydel, but someone who was used to Spanish names might."

Liz said, "We might find out if this Foster is the kind to hire unidentified Mexicans."

Landon nodded. "We might. I'm ready to grasp at almost any straw. I've been out of town about as long as I can manage—not that I particularly need the money. But I have a business reputation of sorts, and I can't afford mysterious disappearances. We might as well go and have a talk with that fellow Foster."

"Mind if I tell Branzell?" Landon shook his head, and Marcus went out. Liz followed him with her eyes, and finally said, "I wish you hadn't brought him into this. I'm not sure I like him."

"Liz, I had no choice. He was in it from the start.

You might as well go and pack. If this is another wild goose chase, I'll fly back to New York, and try to work out a new approach. If we don't find them in a week or so, we never will."

"Well, do we have to take Marcus along?"

Landon stood with his hands clasped behind his back. "I suppose not, but he might try some hunting on his own. I'm nervous."

"Some special reason? Or are you mind reading again?"

Landon laughed sourly; he'd give a lot to read Marcus' mind. "No, but I have hunches sometimes. Right now, one hunch is telling me to get rid of Marcus fast, but another hunch is riding me, telling me to keep an eye on him. Between the two he's less trouble where I can watch him." He smiled at the girl. "I think sometimes you're the only sane person around. I couldn't live without you."

Her answering smile was crooked. "You pay me well."

He turned, his voice going hoarse. "Liz, don't! I'm—even after thirty years here, I'm not wholly free. You know I'm a sort of—of soldier—"

"And regulations include no fraternizing with the natives?"

"Liz!" He gripped her shoulders. "That's not fair!"

"I notice you don't say it isn't true." She removed his hands, firmly and almost forcibly, from her arms. "And if we're not going to get rid of Marcus, let's go and pick him up."

Clearwater lay almost three hundred miles from the Branzell ranch, a small town near San Angelo, with a single small street, the inevitable water tower straddling the town, head and shoulders above the roofs. They located the Foster Cotton Company and Landon left Liz and Marcus in the car while he went in to talk to Foster.

He told a qualified truth. "I read about your bull in the papers. I thought it might make a good feature story—good publicity for your herd, too."

Foster's eyes were not friendly, though he was civil enough. "Thanks, but the less publicity of that kind, the better. Once word gets around that a stud animal is vicious, his value drops."

"The fellow who stopped the bull—was he one of your regular cowhands?"

Foster shook his head. "No, just a wetback. Only been here two, three weeks." Landon kept his face noncommittal, but the time element was right. "I never gave him a second look till the other evening. He's not quite all there, I'd say. After it happened, he claimed the other fellow, his brother I guess, hypnotized the bull. We get some awful dumb ones."

"You don't suppose he really hypnotized it?"

To Landon's surprise, Foster hesitated and said, "You never can tell. That brother of his was a queer one. Hunchback. I put him to work as a checker, and come to think of it, that's peculiar. I usually give that job to someone I know real well. It's too easy to cheat on it. But he gave me the impression he was plumb honest." He looked up, almost but not quite laughing. "You don't reckon he hypnotized me?"

He added, "About the bull business, I couldn't say. I was flat on my face in the dust, expecting the critter to stomp me. Everybody says it was some stunt, though."

Landon tried to make his next question offhand.

He told himself, sternly, that this Reydel might turn out to be, simply, a young Mexican with a talent for amateur rodeo work; but he was inwardly convinced that the long hunt was over.

"Where could I find young Reydel?"

"Well, now," Foster said slowly, "I haven't the least notion. This morning they didn't come out with the other pickers. And my foreman, Vincente, told me that Reydel and his whole family just packed up and left."

For a moment Landon's disappointment was so acute that he let his pose of disinterest slip.

"Why?"

Foster demanded reasonably, "How the hell would I know?" and Landon, shaken, murmured a few noncommittal commonplaces and left. But as he walked out to the car he felt as if he had had a body blow.

Now he was positive of the identity of the supposed Reydels. It was just what the Dvanethy conditioning against betraying their past would prompt them to do.

He returned to the car and sat there despondent. Finally Liz, troubled by his silence, leaned over to lay a consoling hand on his arm. "Weren't they the ones?"

"I don't know. I'll probably never know." He told the story in a few words, finishing, "We're sunk. I could chase them all over Texas for the next ten years."

Ned Marcus suggested, "I could give their description to the highway police, and have them arrested for robbery. That way we'd get a description of them on the wires—"

"Good God, no!" Landon refused emphatically. "What could we say when the police did catch them? And they have no identification papers. Unless I explained everything, which I can't, they'd just be illegal entrants to this country, and the authorities would just deport them. At least, in Texas, I can hunt for them as a citizen. I'd have no excuse to do detective work in Mexico." He glanced at his watch. "Well, if I drive like hell, I can just about make the evening plane to New York."

"You're giving up?"

"Not yet," Landon said, "but there are a few things in New York I have to take care of." Vialmir, he was thinking, would be waiting impatiently for a report. "Liz, can you hold down this end for a few days?"

"Are you counting me in?" Marcus asked.

Landon hesitated. He really had nothing against the youngster except a vague hunch, and the annoying shuttlethinking, which wouldn't bother Liz. "It's up to Miss Curran," he said at last.

Liz searched Landon's face, but found no hint there.

"He'd recognize Mathis and Reidel," she said at last. "Yes, let him come."

"All right." Marcus listened to what little Landon had learned from Foster—that the elusive Reydel had bought Vicente's rattletrap truck, and that they had been seen to drive away on the San Angelo highway.

"Let me get to a telephone. I want to tell Steve what I'm doing and where I'll be."

Landon was airborne over Cleveland before he realized that Ned Marcus had not accounted to him for the radiobromine residue.

9

RESTLESSLY, Cleta turned over the contents of the cardboard boxes containing the few things they had brought when they left the barracks.

In the other room of the quiet tourist cabin she heard the argument still going round and round, just as it had been when Cleta walked out on it. Reidel's stubborn voice, "On the Foster place we were expected to act like foreigners. Here we don't know what to expect!"

And Arran's voice, rising angrily over the rest, "Maybe when we landed you had to take charge, but do you have to keep making our decisions all our lives?" A door slammed and Arran came into the room. "What are you doing, Cleta?"

"The things from the lifeship have to be destroyed. I thought you'd done it already. It's a Dvaneth law."

"Dvaneth law!" Arran made a derisive sound. "The Federation isn't wasting any worry on us. We're dead, as far as they know. What right have they to dictate to us?"

"I wish you'd destroy the shockers, at least."

"The shockers are just what I intend to keep." Arran slipped one into his pocket. "Not that I couldn't make one in an hour or two, given proper materials. Simplest thing in the world!"

He came closer to her, taking her arm and turning her around; his eyes were fierce with eager-

ness. "Cleta, this planet—hell, I could own it!"
This barbarian backwater—internal combustion
engines, no less! Just one step above the invention
of the wheel. I could rip one apart blindfold! And
that's typical of the place. Listen—" He bent his
eyes on her. "Reidel talks caution, caution, but I
can give you the kind of life you really deserve,
and it won't be long, either. Say you'll come with
me!"

The girl stared at him, half amused but as his
strong young arms swung her around and pris-
oned her, she became aware that it was no joke.

"Please, Arran—"

"Is that what you want, Cleta?" Reidel asked
from the doorway. Shaved, dressed neatly in a
new grey work shirt and jeans, he looked less the
roughneck, more the professional man he had
been; but now he looked weary and grim. Cleta
struggled for some word of excuse, but speech
always deserts a telepath in the grip of strong
emotion, and she sobbed, sick with shame, unable
to push Arran away.

Reidel ignored her, trying to control blazing
jealousy. Was he a civilized man, or a damned
barbarian? "Foster had a proposition for me," he
said quietly. "He wanted me to go with a rodeo—
that's an exhibition of horses—as a trainer. I never
considered it seriously, because the rest of you felt
it important we should drop out of sight. And to
me it seemed important that we should stay together."

Cleta found her voice, and said thickly, "I know
we have to stay together. I'm sorry, Reidel, so
sorry."

"Nothing to be sorry about." He pushed past
her and drank a glass of water with thirsty haste,

as if nothing else mattered. The telepathic girl picked up his thought, *I don't own her.*

"I'm no dictator. You gave me my way, Arran; now I'm willing to take yours."

"It isn't my way," the youngster said exasperated. "It's what's best for all of us."

"No matter," Reidel sat down, his head bent. "You're in charge."

The first step of Arran's plan was to get rid of Vicente's truck; it could be too easily traced and was little more than junk anyway. But driving through the desultory traffic, Reidel was silent, his shoulders drawn taut. "We should have brought Mathis."

"Use your head!" Arran snapped. "His picture was in the paper and he's too easily identified by looks. Do you think we need a telempath to outwit anybody on this backwater planet?"

Reidel felt desperately uneasy. Arran was underestimating the world on which they had landed. "Their technology may not be up to ours," he protested, "although we haven't really seen enough of it to know. But even so, it wouldn't mean they were lacking in intelligence."

Arran didn't answer, and Reidel gave up. He only hoped they wouldn't find out, the hard way, that he was right.

They had located a used car lot, tucked under the approaches of a bridge, and Arran drove through the gate under the little fluttering pennants that spelled out WE BUY AND SELL. They got out, and a salesman came toward them.

"Can I help you?"

Reidel barely listened, looking round the rows of used cars, while Arran talked to the man. He had given up his leadership, he told himself; he wouldn't interfere. Arran had produced the title and registration papers. He had been careful to ask Vicente about the necessary transfers to property. The salesman glanced over them.

"Arran Reydel, eh? You look a bit young, and I don't see a parent's counter signature on these. Are you legally of age?"

Arran did not wholly understand, but tried to cover ignorance with annoyance. He said, "Of course," and hoped it were true; he hadn't the slightest idea what the legal age was on this planet. The man handed back the papers.

"Maybe we can do business, but I'll have to telephone. Wait here." He indicated a wooden bench and went inside, closing the office door; Arran sat down, but Reidel remained standing.

"We're in trouble, Arran. You've no driver's license either. Can't you see how little we really know about this place, if a simple thing trips us up like this, without Mathis to probe and interpret for us?" A rudimentary instinct in Reidel was warning him to get away from there fast; but Arran, less sensitive than Reidel (like all animal experts, Reidel was a partial empath) did not understand that the older man was sensing the full blast of the salesman's suspicions.

"We can bluff our way through anything. Relax, Reidel. Don't let these people scare you." He grinned, stretching out his long legs. "And if we can't bluff—" he patted his pocket. Reidel stared at him in dismay, not knowing what he meant, but sensing the menace in his thoughts. His skin prickled. He turned uneasily and saw a black-and-white car sliding up to the curb and two uniformed men crossing the sidewalk. One of them came quietly, but purposefully, toward Arran and

Reidel; the other bent to look at the license place of Vicente's rattletrap truck.

"That's it," he said quietly.

The second policeman snapped out at Reidel "*Come se llama? A dónde vive? Dónde han ustedes trabajado??*"

Lying didn't come naturally to Reidel, and without Mathis at hand he blurted out the truth. "We worked for Nick Foster, in Clearwater."

"It figures," said the second man. "We've picked up wetbacks from that Foster outfit before this." He said in Spanish, "Do me the favor of showing your work card, if you please."

Reidel stood mute. He knew they had none of the necessary credentials. The officer said quietly, "I'm sorry, but you'll have to come with me."

Arran glanced wildly around and his fists clenched. "Reidel! Are you going to let this—this—" Words failed him. His hand slid into his pocket and came out clutching the shocker. Reidel by sheer conditioned reflex flung himself on Arran, fighting down the boy's arm. He rabbit-punched Arran's arm muscle, grabbing the shocker from the suddenly limp hand, and with one swift movement broke it open and crushed the essential part of the mechanism under his heel.

Then there was a rough, restraining grip on them both. "What was that?" demanded Arran's captor, roughly and efficiently running his hands over the boy's body in search of other weapons.

Reidel caught at a random excuse.

"A—a toy—he thought he could frighten you with it—"

The policeman glanced at the broken plastic thing in Reidel's hand and shrugged. "Drop it, then. And you—" he gave Arran a shove, "no more of that. We can put you in handcuffs if you want to get rough."

In the police car Reidel sat silent, shoulders sagging. He knew Arran blamed, and would always blame him for their failure to escape with the shocker, but he was too frantic with worry to waste thoughts on Arran. What would happen to the women? From Vicente's talk, he knew that anyone who crossed the border without a permit was summarily deported. But where, and how far?

At the police station they were searched more thoroughly, and Reidel's knife was confiscated; then they were conducted to a cell. As the steel door banged, Arran said, speaking Dvanethy in his horror, "Reidel, we haven't committed a crime, have we?"

Reidel was fighting down hysteria himself. "I thought I'd mention the women—we'd at least be deported together, what are countries and boundaries to us here?—but we can't have them brought to a place like *this!*" On Dvaneth, where civil offenders were placed in house arrest and criminals sent to readjustment centers and hospitals, the stigma of a place of actual confinement was horrible and lifelong; it meant a place for hardened, brutal incorrigibles, past all redemption.

Arran flung a gutter obscenity at Reidel. "Why didn't you let me use the shocker, you—"

Reidel kept his voice as calm as he could. "We couldn't have disposed of them all. And if they'd found it wasn't made on this world, we'd have had trouble."

"I suppose we're not in trouble now!" Arran dropped his face in his hands, and in shock and pity Reidel realized that the cocky youngster was fighting childish sobs. Reidel laid a hand on his shoulder, trying to convince himself as well. "Mathis will look after the women. Meanwhile, the less trouble we make, the less trouble we'll have. Why don't you try and get some sleep?"

And finally Arran, being young, did sleep. But Reidel did not close his eyes that night.

10

In Landon's New York apartment, the clock face was swung aside, and Landon, leaning forward before the thing that could have been a mirror and wasn't, might have been adjusting his tie.

—*Clannon.*

—*Vialmir here. Make your report.*

—*I found the usual implosion residue. A Dvanethy lifeship.*

—*Not Rhu'inn dominated? Are you sure, Clannon?*

—*How can I be sure?* In thought swifter than speech, the man called Landon outlined his search and Vialmir replied swiftly.

—*You must find the survivors. There might be a Rhu'inn-sensitive among them. Clannon, even using the augmentator like this is dangerous if there should be Rhu'inn on this planet. It could draw their attention.*

Landon felt the stiff short hairs at the back of his neck bristling with atavistic horror. The Rhu'inn. The enigma of the universe. They had nothing resembling normal senses. Most of their perceptions seemed to lie in some register of vibration outside humanly perceptible wave lengths. As regarded the material world, they were blind, deaf, and invisible. They seemed to have no notion of sight or sound, touch or smell.

Their technology—if technology was the word

for anything so unsubstantial—was largely extrasensory. They had only one field or overlap with humans—the two senses of telepathy and empathy. There human met Rhu'inn on fairly even terms, with one exception. Anything a human telepath could do with the Federation's carefully developed apparatus—augmentators, telepathic dampers—the Rhu'inn could do better without them.

—Could Rhu'inn live here without revealing themselves?

—I don't have to remind you that Rhu'inn can use human hosts. Vialmir's thought was grim.

—If there were a telempath among the survivors, is there any chance of finding him mentally without locating him physically, Vialmir?

—It's not impossible. Landon mentally pictured the high, almost inaccessible mountain crag in Tibet where Vialmir lived. He could not have survived more than a short time in the thick oxygen atmosphere of sea level on this planet.

—Some of my people here are good functioning telepaths; after all, they've been our contacts on Earth for centuries. They call the Rhu'inn devils, but that's true enough. I could get them all into the augmentator for a search. It would be dangerous, but this is a Closed Planet, and we're all expendable by definition.

—We could try it as a last resort, I suppose— Suddenly the sensitive mechanical-telepath shrieked soundlessly, with pure horror.

RHU'INN! HELP US!

The shock was so violent that Landon physically staggered, with agony poking every nerve in his body and brain. Then it all went dark and blind and vanished.

When sight came back, Landon found himself sprawled on his face on the carpet, a picture burned into his brain. He could examine it only in momory, for Vialmir had vanished like a blown-out flame, and Landon could not reactivate the augmentator; for all he could tell, Vialmir might be dead, shocked mindless by that blasting force.

The picture was of a large room somehow bare and crowded, with a blaze at the center that could have been fire or a brain-blinding mental focus of force. There was nothing intangible about tele-pathy. It was just as palpable as electric power, and some frequencies were deadly; they could vibrate their harmonics into the magnetic field of an entire planet.

Someone—a trained telepath or telempath, no untrained mind could project such a force—had mentally shrieked for help; and that cry had shown up on the augmentator like a jet streaking across a radar screen. And then, belatedly, Landon realized that it hád all been superim-posed, like a double exposure, on the face of Ned Marcus.

Ten minutes later the augmentator had been stripped to component parts, scattered into boxes of assorted radio and electronics equipment, and Landon, with no luggage but his hat, was speed-ing toward the airport.

"You'll have to accept it," Mathis said at last. "They're not coming back."

The sun of the third morning was sending fierce light through the blinds of the tourist cabin; even Dionie had abandoned the pretense of optimism.

"But what could have happened?"

Mathis said, "They might have broken some law without knowing it. They might have been hurt." He cursed his own double sensitivity; the emotions of the women, tearing at him, made his words harsher than he intended. "Or they might have deserted us."

Cleta's heart-shaped face was white with shock. "They wouldn't!"

"Arran wanted to leave us and strike out on his own the first evening," Mathis said wearily. "Reidel talked him out of it—that time."

"I can't believe Reidel would leave us," Cleta repeated.

"It's your fault!" Dionie pounced on Cleta like a small and gusty hurricane. "You were always belittling Reidel, fighting him! He hated you!" Her voice was high and hysterical; suddenly she broke into frantic sobs and fled into the other room. Cleta, rising in shocked protest, took a step or two after her; but Mathis, moving with unusual swiftness, gripped her arm and held her back.

"You'd only make things worse." He signed to Linnit, with an imperative jerk of his head, to follow the sobbing Dionie. As Linnit picked up the baby and obeyed, Mathis added "Besides, I want to talk to you."

But when they were left alone he did not speak for some time, regarding Cleta in silence; and at last it was Cleta who broke it.

"Mathis, what is the extreme range of a telempath's perception?"

The dwarf hesitated, then shrugged. "I've never tried to find out, though I may have to, before this is over. Neither Reidel nor Arran has more than rudimentary psi; but still, knowing them as well as I do, I ought to be able to contact them at any reasonable distance. I've tried. As far as I can tell, they're not within ordinary perceptive range at all." He hesitated. "How much telepathic training have you had, Cleta?"

"Not much. Why?" But she could read his unspoken thought.

If disaster, not desertion, kept Reidel and Arran away from us, then there may be some great danger here, some danger we should know about.

He said aloud, "Perhaps you and I, in rapport, could reach other telepaths on this planet. I've tried—more or less at random—but so far, I've only found two. One wasn't sane. The other was a child just learning to walk, and mentally defective. The proportion of telepaths on this world must be astronomically low. There are plenty of empaths, but without special training they can't receive worded thoughts."

He looked straight at her adding, "That's Dionie's trouble, of course."

Cleta did not want to think about that. She asked, "Why do you want to find other telepaths?"

"Because they'd believe us, Cleta. No one else would. And another thing—in a world with such a small proportion of telepaths, it's possible that the more intelligent, sane, adjusted ones might band together—probably in some form of secret society. They may even have had some contact with the Federation, through the Watcher here. But the main thing is—they'd believe us, and they'd help us find him."

Cleta nodded. It sounded reasonable. She dropped into rapport with Mathis; and slowly, carefully, extending the net of contact thread by thread, they sent out questing feelers of thought.

It was nightmarish. Cleta was so unaccustomed to keeping her mind open that within minutes she was a bundle of raw screaming nerves. Bits of irrelevant thought filtered randomly from everywhere, but never once did she contact the familar flow-and-response of mutual telepathic contact. Once she touched a shuttlethinker, and the contact was so painful that she gasped aloud, shattering the rapport; it was like scraping a burned finger across sandpaper.

Mathis laid a steadying hand on her shoulder. "How close?"

"I don't know!" Cleta shrank from that contact again, and Mathis studied her uneasily.

"You're worn out. We'll try again later."

"Mathis, this random searching isn't accomplishing a thing. It would make more sense to try and trace how Arran and Reidel left the city—trains, bus stations and so forth. You could probe and see if anyone there had seen them."

"*Bus station*," Mathis repeated, staring at Cleta with such intensity that she flinched. "You may have picked up something, Cleta; I kept getting that, too."

He rose. "Get a coat, it's cold."

The bus station was big and bleak and Cleta hesitated at the doors, curiously unwilling to step inside. Mathis looked back impatiently, and she conquered her unease and followed the small twisted figure through the crowds.

Almost immediately she focused on the center of her discomfort. Standing near a row of baggage lockers stood a tall, dark young woman—and the young man who had discovered them, in the field, the morning after the crash.

The man raised his head and his eyes rested thoughtfully on Mathis. Cleta, sensing a sudden, rude mental touch, flung out a telepathic slap and met perfect, locked defense.

She gripped Mathis' arm, panicky. "Mathis, over there—isn't that the same man who—careful. he's a shuttlethinker!" She had whispered it aloud. A low voice was inaudible unless you were within hearing range, while telepathic contact was as open as a shout, if another telepath happened to be within the perceptive field.

Mathis looked up; then, abruptly, harshly, "It's not the same man! It's *not*! It can't be even a—"

He stopped. And then—

Then Cleta became aware of sudden tremendous tension; like a glare, a frightening grip, a sort of mental smell. Fear spurted inside her ribs.

Rhu'inn!

Rhu'nn! The word vibrated madly in her brain, with a sudden surge of words in a terrifying, familiar language.

—Where are you? Where are you? We can't do anything to help unless we know. . . .

All this. Battering her mind, impossibly amplified, not in their own Dvanethy dialect but in the Standard which every Federation citizen learned. She kept herself upright with an effort that made her heart pound and pound, but a maelstrom of confused pictures flooded, swirling, in her mind—a skyline of tall buildings, a line of mountain crags, irrelevantly Kester's smashed chest and dead face, the dark young woman by the baggage lockers, the flat surface of an augmentator which would be found only in the keeping of a highly trained telepath.

Horror surged away like a wave receding at low tide. How long Cleta had stood unconscious, unseeing, she never knew. The girl, and the familiar-strange man, were gone. Mathis had slumped down on a wooden bench, breathing painfully. With an effort that made sweat start from his face, he muttered, "Close down—wide open—only thing saved us, they didn't dare attract attention—"

Outside in the street the high scream of a siren began and went wailing way, and Mathis twitched in terror.

"See what happened!"

Cleta was sick with fear at the thought of opening to that horror again, but as she probed briefly for contact with someone, the blessed normality folded round her like a blanket. A busy mother shushed a crying child; a man in uniform, head pillowed on a rucksack, dozed on one of the benches; an old lady in long-sleeved black stared with purse-mouthed disapproval at Cleta's bare arms. Cleta was too relieved at the calm normality of the thought to resent it.

"A woman fainted on the sidewalk; they're taking her to a hospital."

Mathis relaxed. "I'm not surprised. If there was a sensitive within a mile of *that*—" His face still looked like death. She sat beside him on the hard bench, shielding him with her body and her mind.

"What happened?"

"I'm not sure." Cleta measured his distress by the fact that he spoke Dvanethy. "All hell's going to cut loose on this planet, Cleta. Someone tried to kill us both—someone who knows Rhu'inn tricks. And someone else tried to get through to us with an augmentator."

Cleta caught her breath. "That means there is a Watcher here!"

Mathis said in an urgent undertone, "Yes, and we've got to find him. It's more, now, than life or death for ourselves. *There are Rhu'inn on this planet!*"

The compulsive memory made Cleta feel sick again. She huddled into her thin coat, looking down at the slumped body of the telempath. She no longer thought of his almost superhuman powers, only his agonizing weakness and frailty. Her eyes widened with delayed shock and she said, "Mathis, what good will it be if we do find the Watcher now? There's no defense against Rhu'inn—none. It's only a matter of time now."

"What a fool you are, Cleta!" Mathis sat upright, and his fierce dark eyes blazed, unquenchable, from his white face. "Do you really think I'd be putting myself through this—this hell, if it were hopeless? Gods of the Galaxy, why do you think they sent ten telempaths in one starship? We were going to a new colony right at the rim of the Forbidden Stars, remember? Haven't you ever heard of the nullifier field?"

"Never," Cleta said.

"We're just beginning to learn about the Rhu'inn. The Rhu'inn don't believe, I think, that a human has any mind worth understanding. Just as—well, some insects have better sight than ours, but we don't take a bug's brain into consideration because of that. Telepathically, the Rhu'inn are as far beyond a human telepath as the telepath is beyond the bug I was talking about. But we've theorized that they sometimes find humans useful because our senses extend into dimensions over which the Rhu'inn have no direct control or perception."

He paused, wondering how to make it clear to her.

"They can take over whole populations, physically and mentally, when they want to. They don't seem to understand why humans should mind that. Fortunately they don't often bother."

He was silent again, while Cleta shivered. Finally he said, "This is top secret, even on Dvaneth, but there is a protection. The nullifier field. I couldn't explain it all, even if I understood it myself—which I don't. But it's already been set up on most of the Federation planets, and its being set up each new colony. Basically, if it's set up within the magnetic field of a planet, it forces the Rhu'inn back into their own dimension."

Mirthless laughter rattled in Mathis' throat. "As far as we know, it doesn't even hurt them—just forces them out of this particular segment of the spacetime universe. Like electric fencing around a stock pen."

"And you understand the nullifier field?"

Mathis hesitated, then qualified. "I couldn't set one up myself. I know the specifications, and if I could find the Watcher, maybe he'd understand it and be able to get access to the materials. Maybe. It sounds hopeless, doesn't it? Especially when you stop to think that the nullifier field is very new, and if the Watcher on this Closed Planet has been here very long, he probably came here long before anyone had ever heard of it. But it's a chance we'll have to take."

"But how do we find him?" Cleta demanded, and Mathis let his eyes fall wearily shut.

"That's exactly the problem."

11

"IT'S LUCKY Miss Curran was carrying my address in her purse," said Steve Branzell. Landon, facing him in the bleak white hospital corridor, demanded, "But what happened?"

"I don't know any more than you do. I got a phone call saying that a Miss Curran was in the hospital here. I tried to phone your apartment in New York, but there was no answer, so I came down here and when I arrived, Sylvia called to tell me you were already in San Angelo, and I only had to call your hotel. Are you psychic?"

Landon didn't answer, for a nurse was beckoning him to the closed door.

Liz Curran's self-sufficient face looked oddly young against the white hospital gown; Landon took her hand as if he were afraid to break it. "My dear, what happened?"

"I don't know." Liz looked frightened. "I can't seem to remember. They told me I fainted in the street." Her dark brows drew together as if in pain.

"I'll never forgive myself for leaving you!" Landon almost said, *leaving you with Marcus*, but held himself back. It might, after all, have been Ned Marcus who sent that screamed mental SOS.

Liz fought to hold her drooping eyelids open, but Landon was reluctant to disturb her with questions. A brisk young intern relieved his anxiety in a few words.

"A mild concussion, and a terrific bruise on her neck, but no fracture. She'll be all right tomorrow."

"No burns?" Landon asked, and the intern stared as if he were a dangerous lunatic and said, "No. No burns."

Outside, Branzell took charge, grasping his arm. "Come on. We're going out for some food. You look like the devil after a night out." He located an excellent restaurant, and while they waited for steaks, Landon asked the major question in his mind.

"Where was Ned Marcus while this was going on?"

"Damned if I know." Branzell sounded annoyed and worried. "He hasn't been in touch with me at all—or with Sylvia either."

That remembered shock of contact was filed in Landon's mind like a photograph; he took it out now and examined it from every side, trying to extract every perception from it.

Item: an unknown telempath had broken in on his contact with Vialmir. A telempath under stress could break in on even a tight augmentation beam, and on a "head-blind" planet, he and Vialmir used the loosest possible hookup.

Item: Liz turned up with concussion and amnesia.

Item: Marcus had disappeared.

Item: the unknown telempath had actually been sensing the presence of Rhu'inn, which did not mean any Rhu'inn had been physically present. The term physically present was almost meaningless anyhow, in speaking of Rhu'inn, their perceptions of space were not human.

With that unsettling ability to follow a train of

thought, Branzell demanded, "Landon, you spoke of our world as a Closed Planet. What does that mean?"

"That it's permantly cut off from the Federation. No one can leave; anyone who comes has to accept permanent exile."

Earth, till now at least, was not a Forbidden Star, where Rhu'inn were known to exist. It was a Closed Planet because it had once been touched by Rhu'inn.

No one knew why. No one knew what obscure motives drew Rhu'inn out of their unknown trans-material universe and into the normal three-dimensional world. No one knew whether they absorbed civilizations from sheer lust of conquest, or the scientific curiosity of the naturalist who puts on a wolfskin to study the pack.

But they came. And so starships destroyed themselves rather than fall into Rhu'inn hands. And planets once invaded were Closed forever. If you met the Rhu'inn on purely physical terms, for instance, encysted in a human host, then you were safe, as long as you knew the host. But if you met them on mental terms, the only thing to do was commit suicide or force them to kill you— fast, so they couldn't use you against your own kind.

Landon swore. He was the Watcher, and that was all he could do. He could watch.

To the Federation—which meant to the wishful thinkers on Dvaneth—he and Vialmir were there to take note of any possible Rhu'inn invasion. But one man, or two, couldn't actually do a thing, in the case of such invasion, without a convenient miracle. While he and Vialmir were alive, all was assumed to be well. If they failed to report, they were presumed dead and replacements sent. If the replacements disappeared too frequently, Earth would be moved from the list of Closed Planets to the list of Forbidden Stars.

How complacently he had accepted his post of weather balloon!

He swore again, morosely. "I've lived here thirty years without realizing that I was only a concession to politics!"

He told Branzell as much as he could without mentioning the Rhu'inn.

Branzell had let his steak get cold while he listened. "Good lord," he murmured at last. "It explains all the legends! Landon, we've got to find them! I've got half a dozen new approaches. You say one of them is a telepath? Sylvia is clairvoyant, I'll bring her down here and let her see if she can contact them. I'll check every service station and used car lot myself, and every hotel, rooming house or tourist court where they might be hiding out." His eyes glowed at Landon and he vowed, "I'll find them if I have to search San Angelo house by house!"

Liz was released from the hospital next morning. Landon had decided, over a sleepless night, that he wouldn't drag her one step further on this chase. The party was getting too rough.

Another thought kept sneaking into the back attics of his brain; Liz or Marcus, or both, willing or unwilling, might be Rhu'inn tools, hosts or dupes. Anything could lie behind Marcus' shuttlethinking. And while Liz seemed transparent, Landon had learned in a hard school not to trust his own emotions.

"I'm sunk," he confessed to Liz, and sank down in the comfortless hotel room chair. "It's the end of the line. I give up. I've got to get back to New York and salvage what's left. Branzell's on the edge of some big grab for publicity—he won't print a fake story, but he believes this one. Ned Marcus has disappeared, and he has the radio-bromine residue. If he tried to run down any leads on his own, or if the FBI cross his trail—and they might—I'm going to have some explaining to do. And in my New York apartment I've got parts of an augmentator and a telepathic damper, among other things."

Also, though he didn't say so, he had to check and see if Vialmir was still alive. If not, and he couldn't find the unknown telempath—well, somehow a message had to be sent, that Rhu'inn were here again.

"Clint, you can't abandon the survivors now!"

Landon reached for Liz, obeying an impulse as irresistable as the moment itself. But before the embrace could complete itself, a surge of icy reality washed over him and a sense of his terrible isolation. He mastered the impulse, but said, in a voice hoarse with all he was repressing, "Liz, you—you're a miracle. Bless you, girl. But I have to get back. Don't worry about them, too much. They'll adapt. I did."

"Did you?" He read condemnation in her dark eyes. She turned away, without looking at him again. "If you're serious, I'll go and make flight reservations."

She was gone long enough for Landon to begin worrying again; but just as his fear was getting the upper hand she returned, with Steve Branzell in tow. Branzell looked jubilant, and Landon felt like pin-pricking that enthusiasm.

"Did you get me a flight, Liz?"

"Not yet," Branzell answered for her. "I want you to wait here for a phone call. And before you get sore at me for meddling—"

Landon advanced on Branzell, and his eyes were terrible, shocked out of caution by stark fear.

"I swear, if you've given me away—*what have you done?*"

"I've done what we should have done weeks ago—days, anyhow," Brancell growled, "instead of sneaking around like an interplanetary Sherlock Holmes. I went on the assumption that you were a respectable businessman, instead of Space Ranger or the Lord High muckety-muck of Mars—"

Landon stared, felt his knees give way and sat down suddenly. "*You mean you don't believe—*"

"Hell, yes," said Branzell, "I'm talking about what you want people to believe. I know people all over Texas. I went to the police chief, gave them your card, showed him the picture in the paper, and said you were trying to locate a couple of distant relatives who might be in the country illegally and who might be in San Angelo. He made four calls at the taxpayers' expense and told me Ray Reydel and Arran Reydel were being held at the border waiting to be deported." He held up a hand, checking Landon's brief exclamation. He suggested you talk to them by phone and if they turned out to be your long-lost grandsons or cousins or whatever, you could meet them there and bring them into the country legally." Branzell shrugged. "I can pull a string or two; you'll have no trouble with permits."

Landon felt stunned by the simplicity of it all. "You think I should do that?"

"*Should,* hell," said Branzell, "I did it already. You'd better be thinking what to say in case this Reydel turns out to be a perfectly ordinary citizen of Mexico with a talent for bull-fighting."

12

LAREDO lay hot, dry and solitary in the noonday glare, and Arran looked round the airport waiting room suspiciously. "You don't suppose it could be a trap?"

Reidel was irritated at himself for sharing Arran's unease. "No. I talked to him myself, yesterday, and he spoke to me in Dvanethy. He—" Reidel broke off, for a man, and a tall dark-haired woman were coming toward them across the room. For a heart-stopping moment Reidel thought the woman was Cleta, then saw the unfamiliar face beneath the dark hair and stopped, sick with disappointment.

At last he found his voice and his nerve. "You're—" he started to say Clannon, "Landon?"

"Reidel!" Even a less sensitive stranger would have sensed the warmth in Landon's handclasp. "Good to see you, at last! You've led me some chase!"

"How did you find us, Watcher?" Arran asked in Dvanethy.

"It's a long story, and if you don't mind we'll speak English—Spanish if you prefer. Also it would be wise to get the formalities over quickly."

Smoothed by Branzell's influence, these were few. They were told to register their addresses, if they stayed in the country more than six months;

then, since neither could produce evidence of recent vaccination, they were turned over summarily to a local doctor for the process, to which Reidel submitted with amused curiosity, Arran with a glowering resentment. If they had been alone, Reidel would cheerfully have hit him.

At last, aboard the northbound plane and in the semi-isolation of rear seats, Landon could tell them, step by step, of the search. With tension gone and the disgrace of imprisonment behind him, Reidel's thoughts reverted to the pattern uppermost in his mind since the lifeship crash.

"It hasn't occurred to me to ask where we're going, Clan—" He caught and corrected himself, "Landon. But shouldn't we try to find the others?"

"I'm sorry," Landon said reluctantly. "My friends are trying to locate them. Just now I think it's wisest to take you to New York with me. But as soon as it's safe and practical, every resource I have will be at your service, to find them."

"By which time," Arran muttered, "they'll be so well hidden that a telempath with a planetary scanner couldn't find them."

Landon frowned at the interpolated Dvanethy words. Reidel said shrewdly, "You're not really asking us. It's an order, isn't it?"

Landon felt uncomfortable. "I wouldn't put it that way. I'm older, and I've more experience here—"

"And resources," Arran muttered.

"You know best, I suppose," Reidel said slowly, "but they're women, and young. I can't help worrying."

"Reidel, there's no use arguing," Arran said. "We're at his mercy."

Landon did not try to answer, knowing nothing could placate Arran's sullen determination to resent everything he said and did. He wondered why. Reidel, too, was inwardly rebellious, but Reidel, at least, was trying to be agreeable.

Landon's apartment had the peculiar quiet of rooms unlived-in for days, but Landon frowned as he stepped inside. It is not difficult for even a rudimentary telepath to sense when someone has been meddling with his things. It could have been a cleaning woman, but Landon suspected the worst. Lately he had turned pessimist.

He took his guests to the spare bedroom and frowned at the neatly stacked mail. Presently Reidel and Arran joined him, washed and brushed and freshly clothed, and Landon gestured.

"Just catching up on the work that piled up while I was away."

"What do you do—when you aren't rounding up strays, that is?"

Landon chuckled. "I don't do much of that. I'm a methods analyst. I set up factory layouts, assembly lines and so forth." He explained in detail, while Arran listened, fascinated, and Landon recalled that this youngster had already reached the Rim Room of a starship. He suggested, "Perhaps you can go to engineering school here. It would give you background, technical vocabulary—"

"Engineering school here?" Arran flung the Dvanethy words like an obscenity. "Anything here, I learned before I was old enough to feed myself with a spoon! Why, they use internal combustion engines! Go to their school?"

Landon gestured him to silence. This was the

time to force a showdown. "Just as you like. However, I must ask one thing, or insist on it as your superior under Dvaneth law—"

Arran's face twisted in derision. "We're a good long way outside the jurisdiction, Watcher."

"Call it a personal favor then. But speak English—or Spanish if you prefer, at all times. Even when you think we're alone. This is the only thing I do ask of you, and it's for my own protection. And my name here is Landon."

His tone silenced Arran completely. Landon started rummaging around the apartment, collecting the scattered boxes of loose parts. "Make yourselves at home. I've a report to make."

Arran came and watched as he spread out his work on the table, his face schooled to indifference. He had had enough of Landon's rebukes for one day. But Landon was aware of his interest.

"I dismantle the augmentator whenever I leave town."

"Do you have—" Arran stopped, then said defiantly, "I don't know the English words!"

Landon said, ready to take advantage of his momentary accessibility, "I can give them to you."

"I could put that together while you do. I've done it any number of times. For my apprentice examination, I had to take apart and rebuild a matrix damper blindfolded."

"Carry on, then." Landon moved aside, and watched the skilled young hands articulating the components, unerringly separating the red-herring junk from the augmentator parts. Arran would have no trouble making a place for himself here, once he'd picked up the rudiments of a technical vocabulary and discarded his arrogant assumption of superiority. Landon, with the technology of two planets at his fingertips, had a solid respect for that of Earth.

They finished, and he activated the augmentator.

The call went unanswered.

Landon frowned, opened the mechanism again and checked Arran's articulation—needlessly, for it was perfect. Again he laboriously calibrated the mechanism and again the call was unanswered.

He waited, his courage dropping to the breaking point. At last he slumped heavily into a chair.

It might mean nothing. Vialmir's augmentator might be out of commission. Or Vialmir otherwise occupied, or ill. Or atmospheric conditions unsatisfactory. But the answer he feared most, seemed most likely; Vialmir had been killed, or shocked out of functioning ability.

Then, at the risk of secrecy, at the risk of all their lives, *Mathis must be found!*

The frail cripple might be this world's only bulwark against unimaginable danger. Telepath and empath, freak of the human race, Mathis was their only defense.

And no one knew where Mathis was.

13

He was debating whether to call Steve Branzell, emphasizing the terrifying urgency of the search now, when there were steps in the hallway and a knock. He swung the clock face shut, gestured to Reidel to open the door, and stood behind him.

He saw two men in the corridor; both in correct grey business suits, both unsmiling and subtly alike though one was tall and thin-faced, the other chubby and slightly bald. The chubby one showed a leather folder.

"Special Investigator Platt, and this is Jorgenson," he said briefly. Landon glanced at the credentials and with unruffled politeness conducted them into the apartment.

"You know why we're here, Landon?"

"I haven't the least idea."

It was the chubby-faced Platt who did the talking. "You recently made a trip to Texas? To the vicinity of the rocket bases there?"

"If I was within a hundred miles of any rocket base, I didn't know it," said Landon, speaking the absolute truth. Present-day rockets were far too inefficient to interest him.

Platt consulted a notebook. "You stayed a month, neglecting some very good business offers. Can you explain?"

Landon leaned against the mantelpiece. "I

don't understand why I have to explain. Is it against the law to neglect my business?"

The trace of a smile flickered on Platt's mouth. "Not unless you go bankrupt. But for the record, what *were* you doing in Texas?"

"Visiting friends. I located some Mexican relatives of mine who were having a rough time, and I brought them back with me."

"I see." Platt snapped his notebook shut and asked with jarring suddenness, "What about radioactive bromine?"

There was a full stop.

Landon's brain was circling wildly, but his manner betrayed nothing except polite interest. "Well, what about it?"

"You'd better not kid around. In the first place—" Platt crossed the room, swung back the clock face and touched the surface of the augmentator, "What is this gadget? We checked this apartment on a call from the FBI, and found it full of loose electronic gadgets."

"Gentlemen," Landon murmured, "electronics is my business."

"Yes. Then we recovered, from a car you've been driving, a jar of code-designated fuel residues—"

Ned Marcus. The name flashed like a red light as Platt continued. "We have some reason to wonder if you are not in contact and communicating with—shall we say, illegal destinations? Do you mind if we search the apartment for a radio transmitter?"

Landon almost laughed, the thought was so absurd. "A transmitter of that power? In an apartment this size? Sure, search away. Are you hiding an atomic furnace in your pocket?" The gaunt Jorgenson snickered, then subsided under Platt's scowl.

"If you find anything resembling a radio—except for an AM-FM portable in the bedroom that I use for listening to news broadcasts and concerts, I'll eat it. As for the augmentator—well, get a radio expert down here to look it over, if you want to."

"No need," Jorgenson said grimly. "I was a radioman in the last war." He approached the augmentator gingerly. "What did you call this mockup?"

"A telepathic augmentator."

"A telewhich?"

Landon spelled it, deadpan.

"Huh," said Jorgenson without inflection. "Looks like a ham operator's nightmare. I won't electrocute myself on it, will I?"

"No cords, no batteries." Landon released the catch of the flat crystal surface, exposing the mechanism inside. The detective knelt, examining the coils and tubes with meticulous care.

"Inspector, what am I supposed to have done? I'm not making a big noise about this, or demanding a search warrant, because as it happens I have nothing to hide. But what am I supposed to have done?"

"I'm not at liberty—" Platt reflected a minute. "This much I can say. A month ago, Civil Defense tracked something on radar which could have been a large meteor or small aircraft. You made a trip to that vicinity and there was a dead man found and the victim, whatever the local police said, was not a Mexican migrant. Analysis of stomach contents proved he hadn't bought his last meal in this country. Then you salvaged and hid coded fuel residue—"

Landon stared. Platt had come so close, yet so frighteningly far from the truth that it was a temptation to tell the whole story. He said, with desperate earnestness, "Is anyone on earth actually using allomorphic bromine for a practical rocket fuel?"

Platt said laconically, "They are now. If you know so much, what happened to the wreckage?"

"There wasn't any," Landon said wearily. "The mechanism was set to destroy the craft on surfacing. It imploded to free neutrons, hydrogen and radioactive carbon—and if you tell me there's any nation on Earth, including the Russians, that's mastered *that* process, you're a fool or a liar."

Jorgenson used an unprintable phrase, stood up and brushed dust from his knees. "Radio! That wouldn't send a radio wave to Flatbush. It's just dummy tubes—glass and fluorite crystals—a fancy fake. Of course," he added slowly, "I couldn't say whether it really does anything, offhand I'd say not, but I wouldn't stake my year's salary on it. I can only say it isn't a radio."

"That's all I wanted to know." Platt turned to go. "You'll be hearing from us, Landon."

"So you'll run back to headquarters," Landon said bitterly, "and when the scientists get through analyzing the crystalline structure of the radio-bromine, and all the red tape has been cut, you'll decide it really wasn't made on Earth. And then, you'll go through some more red tape and ask me what I know, and then—" his voice was savage now, "you'll call a session of psychiatrists to decide whether or not to believe me. And by then it will be too late."

Platt only repeated, "You'll be hearing from us."

When they had gone, Landon sank in a chair and buried his head in his hands. Reidel stood beside him, looking distressed. "I hate to think we've gotten you into trouble."

Landon sighed. "It's not your fault. I'd have had to locate the implosion residue, even if you'd all died in the crash. But do you realize what it means—if Earth is using radiobromine now?"

"Well," Arran wanted to know, "what else is there to use?"

"That's exactly the point. There's been no real space travel here because they've been working on the wrong lines for fuel—inefficient, fabulously expensive stuff. But if they've discovered the allotropic bromine, that means they're in—or rather, they're out, they're loose. Not interplanetary travel—interstellar! They might flounder a while, but it would be a year or two, at most.

Now, somehow, over incredible obstacles if Vialmir was dead, a message had to get through. This particular Closed Planet was no longer safely isolated by inability to get past its own dead moon. But before he made much progress explaining this, there was another knock on the door.

"Now what?" Landon demanded, tempted not to answer it at all. Then, on the off chance that it might be Liz Curran, he went and opened the door. Ned Marcus was standing in the hallway.

"Hell," said Landon in disgust, "you again?" He started to slam the door, but Marcus caught and held it.

"Hold on! I owe you an explanation, I guess. Listen, I had to save my own neck. The FBI picked me up for questioning about that killing, and they found that radioactive gook in the back of my car.

So I told them it was something of yours. What else could I do? They were talking about crashed Russian test aircraft, and fuel stolen from Cape Canaveral."

Landon glared, then abruptly became aware they were still standing in the doorway. "Come inside, then. I'm not going to stand here in the hall, and argue."

Marcus came in, and looked at Reidel with a glance of mutual recognition. "Why get sore at me, Landon? You found them anyway, I see."

And Landon's thoughts recoiled again, flatly, from the shuttlethinking surface.

He was sure it was deliberate. The ordinary nontelepath is vulnerable to any telepath who speaks his language and can prod the right mental trigger. But Marcus was oblivious to the roughest mental force Landon could use, short of murder.

Marcus meanwhile, seeming totally oblivious to the rough mental assault, was talking casually to Reidel and Arran about the search. "Is Miss Curran all right? She fainted on the street, and I took her to a hospital; that was where the FBI caught up with me again. Listen. Can't you prove the whole thing by giving the FBI the formula for that fuel?"

Landon stared, finally laughed.

"I'm an administrator, not a spaceman. I probably know less about spaceships and fuels than you do! But even if I knew, I'm not allowed to interfere in the internal affairs of this planet. Giving any one nation technological advantages over any other—"

"Even when that one nation is maintaining world peace?"

Landon shrugged. "Go wave your flag somewhere else."

Arran broke in, "But, I do know the fuel formulas, Clannon! If you could—"

Landon swung away from Marcus, deadly menace in his eyes.

"No! Not even to save my life or yours! Dvaneth law absolutely forbids any Closed Planet to be given such things."

"They'll get it anyway from that residue," Arran blurted, "and according to that detective, they're discovering it themselves!"

Landon looked troubled, for Arran was perfectly right. "If I could contact Vialmir and get authorization—"

"Can't you do anything under your own initiative?" Arran asked, with a shadow of contempt.

Landon said a flat, final, "No."

Marcus was looking speculatively at Reidel and Arran. "If nothing else I could help these two get acquainted with the city," he said. Then, with a shrewd glance at Arran, he said the one thing calculated to cut off Landon's possible objections at their source.

"Or don't you trust them out without you?"

When he put it that way there was nothing Landon could say. His guests were old enough to take care of themselves, and guests, not prisoners. Marcus had to be accepted at face value, or else faced down and outmatched.

In a way it was a relief to see the three young men leave.

14

THE LECTURE hall was deserted at this hour, a bleak grey room with tables marred by hundreds of absent-minded pencils.

Ned Marcus, scribbling hasty figures, glanced at Arran and the boy took the pencil and turned the paper to sketch quickly, "I don't know your terminology. But you coat the—the coil with the special damping compound, or the reaction gets back to your hand and paralyzes it—"

Reidel scowled and hit the table with his fist. "I don't like this!"

"What else can we do?" Arran asked. "Clannon's fumbling like a blind worm; he simply doesn't realize there's no time for his methods. I can redesign and rebuild a shocker. His government can't call us cranks if we have something to demonstrate."

"The internal affairs of this planet—"

"Once for all," Arran yelled, "we are *outside* Dvaneth law! Landon means well, but he's been conditioned to hopeless inefficiency and it's time somebody woke him up!"

"I have a friend on the faculty here," Marcus added. "It's a chemistry lab, not electronics, but I thought it would be better because of that atomic weights chart."

Arran rose and examined it. "The symbols are different, and the drawing, of course," he said,

"but it's the same old periodic table of elements."
He came back to check the equipment piled on the
demonstration table.

"Heat equipment, clamps and tongs, wire.
Copper wire won't work if we're going to step this
up to a lethal charge. We could fudge up a demonstration model with copper, but we should
have—" He stepped back to the chart, ran his
finger down the atomic weights of metals, and
Marcus translated where his finger pointed.

"Iridium, tungsten, silver—there might be
silver wire in the medical building; they use it in
surgery. What else?"

"Silicon powder or silicon paper, quartz crystals and equipment for cleaving them. We can get
that next door."

Reidel pretended to be sleepier than he was. He
laid his arms on the table, dropping his head into
them, and heard their footfalls die away.

He raised his head and looked around. Smash-
ing or interfering with their equipment wouldn't
delay them long; anyway, it didn't belong to Marcus and he didn't suppose the laws against van-
dalism changed much from planet to planet. Arran's diagram of the shocker lay on the bench.
Reidel turned it over in his hands. He couldn't
make head or tail of it. He crumpled it into his
pocket and went. If he had them figured right,
they'd pay no more attention to his absence than
his presence.

He walked in on Landon like a black thun-
dercloud, forcing the paper into his hands.
Landon untangled it and let out a low whistle of
dismay.

"And a lethal calibration figured on it. The
damn fools!" Grim mouthed, he flug it down.

"We've got to stop them!" He crossed the room, pulled open a drawer and took out an automatic. He checked it, and put it into his pocket.

"You'd better know," he said, as he scribbled a few lines on a card, "that I'm prepared to kill them both before I let this happen. If I'm killed myself, or arrested, take this to Steve Branzell. It explains how to use the augmentator. Find Mathis if you can; if not, tell Branzell what you know, and let him decide."

He started to leave. "I'm coming too," Reidel said grimly, "Arran's my responsibility."

The lecture room was locked now, no light penetrating beneath the closed door. Landon bent and touched the lock with one finger; after a minute Reidel heard the mechanism snap back, and the door swung open. Landon was breathing more heavily than usual.

"I didn't know I could still do that. But they've gone. You didn't hear their plans?"

"No." Reidel swore. "I should have stayed—"

"No, they wouldn't have discussed anything definite in front of you, once you'd formulated your objections. I'll bet Marcus is a telepath behind that shuttlethinking. But let's get out of here before they arrest us for breaking and entering."

They cut, in silence, across the deserted city block that was the college campus. Landon muttered, "I should have probed Arran's mind when he first started arguing with me. I'd like to get Marcus under the augmentator, but it's too big a risk—"

"Clint—" Reidel began.

"If you have any questions, Reidel, save them! I have enough unanswered ones right now. But if you have any bright ideas, for goodness sake, let's have them."

"Just where, exactly, are we heading?"

Landon stopped short. Exactly nothing would be gained by wandering around Brooklyn at midnight, with a loaded gun in his pocket.

"There's an automat down the street. Let's talk that over."

The automat was the first really familiar thing Reidel had seen on this planet. They took coffee and amorphous-looking hunks of pie, and carried them to a table. Reidel looked doubtful.

"Can we talk here?"

"When you have private business, take it to a public place. The more crowded the better," said Landon, stating Rule One in a life of successful camouflage. Reidel put a fork in his pie, while Landon finally forced himself to face the possibility he had been avoiding; that Liz, or Marcus, or both, were working with Rhu'inn. He tried to explain to Reidel and got nowhere.

"I thought Rhu'inn weren't human!"

"I mean carrying one as a parasite."

"But why? People don't just join up with nonhumans against humanity."

Landon stared at the tabletop, turning that over in his mind. What could prompt a man to join up with man's oldest enemy? He saw that Reidel was gripping his fork till the knuckles popped white.

"Do you—are you thinking Arran could be—"

Landon said an instant, unequivocal, "Hell, no. At least not yet. Your friend Mathis couldn't possibly have lived under the same roof with him for weeks, or for more than a few hours, without one of them suspecting and killing the other."

Reidel sighed with relief, and Landon went on,

thoughtfully, "Of course Rhu'inn are incomprehensible by human standards. Marcus—if it is Marcus—would be convinced that his motives are purely altruistic. He's intensely patriotic, though in a distorted way. Maybe all his life he's secretly thought the world would be better off if taken over by an intelligent ruling caste. His education's been lopsided—technical, with no compensating balance in humanities." Suddenly he didn't want to talk about it any more. "Let's get going."

Reidel kept back his questions, but he was not surprised when they rang a doorbell and Liz Curran came into the vestibule of the tiny apartment. Her eyes widened when she saw them.

"Good lord, don't you know it's after midnight? Come in, but be quiet, the old biddies here would love to spread the story that I entertain men at this hour. What's happened?"

She closed the door after him. A dark tailored robe was wrapped high about her throat, and her face, innocent of lipstick, looked pale and strained. "Let me get dressed, Clint, and make some coffee. I need it, if you don't."

Landon said, "I've got to do something I should have done when this first started. I want both of you to let me make a full telepathic examination. Reidel, you first."

He had good reason for that. Reidel was used to such procedures on Dvaneth; his matter-of-factness might make it seem less bizarre for Liz.

"Any time," Reidel said, but his fists knotted, gripping the arm of the chair.

"Relax," Landon said aloud, "it's normal to think of everything you'd like to hide, everybody does. But I'm not interested in your private life." Just the same he slid his hand into the pocket with the automatic. But after a moment the ringing pressure lightened. "Clear. Liz?"

This, of course, was what he had been dreading. The probe of Reidel had been waste motion for her benefit, but now it had narrowed, shockingly, to Liz or Marcus; and it wasn't fair or safe to assume it had to be Marcus; Liz had collapsed; and any major telepathic shock, including the touch of Rhu'inn, would bring on such a period of disorientation.

Liz Curran's face was completely drained of color.

"No," she said in a whisper. "I'm not some—some alien monstrosity, but I won't—" She turned and fled, a sob hanging in the air behind her. The men stared at one another, Reidel mute with distress, Landon, in an agony of suspicion and misery, gripping the pistol in his pocket. Then Liz, shaken and red-eyed, reappeared.

"All right, Clint. Then get the hell out of my apartment and out of my life."

"Liz, I hate to do this to you—"

"That's easy to say, isn't it?" Her shoulders were shaking with the violence of her suppressed sobs. Reidel was shivering, too, with the backlash of transferred emotion before Landon lifted a haggard face.

"You're clear, Liz. I'm sorry about this."

The woman's lips barely moved. "Satisfied?"

"Liz—oh, my dear, my dear—"

She struck his arm down. "I'm not your dear," she said, and now her rigidity began to be shaken by violent trembling. "You—you can't do this to me too—"

Landon's arms were around her now. He said huskily, "I'd never have had the nerve to say it.

I'm not . . ." His words trailed into incoherence. She sobbed wildly for a moment, then dug her face into his shirt front; Landon gently put his hand under her chin, lifted her face and kissed her.

Reidel got up, helplessly and muttered, "I'm going out in the kitchen and make that coffee for you." But neither of them noticed his going.

At three in the morning, the phone rang. Liz, very subdued now, snuggled within the curve of Landon's arm, reached for it and said, "Hello?" and another startled, "Hello? Good grief, do you know what time it is? Well, as a matter of fact, he and Reidel are here." Then she covered the mouthpiece with her hand.

"It's Branzell. He says he's been calling your apartment every hour all night, and called me as a last resort. He's found Mathis and the rest, and they're about to board a plane for New York—"

Landon caught the phone from her hand.

"Steve? You found—yes, yes, no time for that now. Is Sylvia with you?" Reidel heard confused sounds from the phone and Landon swore. "I don't give a damn if you do have to hold up the plane. Steve, this is no time to be funny! Life or death? I wish it was half as simple as life or death! You get Sylvia to this phone, and you get her here damn fast!"

Liz stared, appalled, for Landon was shouting, his face white and distorted. But after a long time he spoke again into the receiver, gently.

"Sylvia? Think carefully, child. Have you ever been able to read your brother's mind?"

Silence. Liz and Reidel exchanged baffled glances.

"Until—recently?" Landon's voice caught; he

actually had to breathe twice between the two words. "Sylvia, listen, when—yes, I know, we call it shuttlethinking, but when did it start?"

Slowly, horror stole across his face. "That day when I first came to the house with him? Yes, I remember, he said, 'No, sis, cut it out. . . .' ' He had to stop and breathe again.

"All right, Sylvia, go and board the plane. But whatever you do—if your brother Ned meets you at the airport, stay away from him, on any excuse whatever. I'll explain when you get here." He hung up, and Reidel said, "He's found them? Found Cleta?"

"And all of them," Landon said, in a voice that made Reidel shrink with dread, "and I almost wish he hadn't."

The taxi seemed to crawl through the jammed streets. Landon held Liz Curran's hand, sharing the short time before the arrival of the others forced duty on him again, and Reidel, watching, understood himself as well.

To Landon, the others were strangers. Landon would do his duty by them, he was even prepared to like them and welcome them as friends from home; but they were strangers. Where as Reidel, through a reluctant acceptance of the duty thrust on him, had formed an indissoluble tie.

The airport was crowded, an orderly confusion that reminded Reidel with nostalgic force of Dvaneth. Uniformed men fussed with rolling steps; Reidel saw Cleta in the door of the plane, and his excitement caught fire. He wanted to shout frantically. Linnit looked tired and cold, the baby a sleeping bundle in her arms. Dionie's eyes sought and found Reidel through the thick crowd;

a strange man had his hand on Mathis' shoulder.
Reidel started toward them when a sudden, shrill
scream, cutting through the noises of the crowd,
touched off a rustle of panic. Dionie threw herself,
still screaming, at Mathis. She wrapped her thin
arms round the dwarf's neck and hurled him to
the ground.

Reidel fought through the crowd, elbowing,
cursing. Somehow he forced his way to them as
Ned Marcus sprang out from behind the baggage
tractor. His hand came up, holding a long tube
from which blossomed a flower of orange flame. It
missed Mathis as he fell in a tangle of Dionie's
arms and legs, and Steve Branzell crumpled with
a cry and crashed down the steps. It seemed to
happen slowly, but in seconds Marcus was brac-
ing the tube for another shot, and Reidel, vaulting
Branzell's fallen body, leaped at him.

He struck up the barrel of the shocker and the
orange flame flared harmlessly in the air. They
collided, and he felt Arran's fist thud into his ribs
as he grappled with Marcus for the shocker.

Someone grabbed him and hauled him bodily
off them. Then a harsh voice rose in deep-throated
authority.

"Drop it! Ladies and gentlemen, please step
back slowly and no one will be hurt. Don't anybody move!"

A queer hush settled down through the muddle
of crowd noises as they edged back, trying to obey
these contradictory orders. Landon saw that the
voice of authority was that of the chubby FBI man,
Inspector Platt; there were blue uniforms everywhere. Handcuffs clinked on Ned Marcus'
wrists; Arran, panting and a little dazed, allowed
himself to be handcuffed to Ned Marcus. Platt

bent for the fallen shocker, then shouted, whirling, "Grab him! Stop him!"

Marcus, still handcuffed, had made a break for freedom, dragging Arran with him. The crowd wavered, streamed back. Platt shouted "Stop him! Shoot to kill!"

"No! Don't kill it," Mathis bellowed, "not in a crowd like this, or we'll all have to die! Can't you see that's what it's trying to make you do?"

Platt shouted; the pistols vanished and Marcus went down in a welter of blue uniforms, dragging Arran down too. He fought blindly. It took a dozen men to subdue him and at a shouted plea from Mathis, whose very hysterical intensity won compliance, to unchain Arran from his wrist.

Arran gave them no more trouble, slumped between the policemen. Marcus too stood beaten at last, hanging almost unconscious between his captors. He had fought so savagely that they had been forced to be brutal, and his face was a mess of bruises and blood. Sylvia screamed when she saw him, and even Landon was sickened by the beating the kid had taken. He had to remind himself that Marcus wasn't just a beaten-up youngster.

Marcus mumbled through swelling lips "Sis . . ."

The FBI man motioned her forward. Sylvia ran toward him, then stopped, stumbled, and a scream of terror ripped her throat. She flung herself on Landon in a frenzy. "Oh, take it away, take it away," she shrieked. "It's not Ned, it isn't, it's not even human, don't let it get me, don't—"

The police had cleared the field now. Platt put a hand on Landon's shoulder.

"We've wasted enough time. You're all under arrest."

As if to underline his words, Liz and Cleta were shepherded politely but firmly toward another waiting police car, while a sturdy police matron approached the hysterical Sylvia, and men ran forward from a hastily summoned ambulance to lift Steve Branzell.

"All of us? On what grounds? You aren't taking the women and children to jail too, are you?"

"Any grounds you please. Assault with a deadly weapon. Undesirable alien. Disturbing the peace if I can't make anything else stick. And we're not taking any of you to jail," Platt told him. "All of you, Landon—or Clannon, if you prefer— are going up river to Albany. And if you want to tell your spaceship story again, this time we'll see if we can't cut a little more of that red tape."

15

LATE the next day, Landon stood before a long roomful of strange faces, unsteadily adjusting the mechanism of the augmentator. His palms were damp, and he wondered half seriously if he should give the calibrator an extra half turn to compensate for the seething anxieties and tensions that were almost an audible vibration in the room.

Beyond the window, against the low hills of the Helderbergs, he could see the WAC barracks where the women had been quartered away from curious eyes. So far there had been little leakage to the press. The riot at the airport had been killed to an inside page. The Army wanted no fantastic rumors of alien weapons and space invaders—and no one else knew that Steve Branzell, partially paralyzed but alive, was recovering in the Base hospital.

Ned Marcus, and for the present Arran too, were locked in maximum-security cells. Mathis, after a full probe, had pronounced Arran clear, but everyone wasn't convinced.

Mathis said, somewhere behind Landon, "You see, as long as Marcus is alive, then as far as we know he's their only physical extension into this dimension. If we keep him isolated, but alive, there isn't much possibility of transfer. But if he should be killed before we get the nullifier established, he might transfer to a host we couldn't identify, and turn all his thoughts to keeping us from getting it set up."

"What I'd like to know," said a uniformed man. "Is where did Marcus get his?"

"I think, from Kester," Mathis said slowly. "We found him unconscious in the lifeship bay. The worst danger of interstellar travel is that the transition from warp to normal space takes place through what we call the Rhu'inn dimension."

"And Marcus found Kester's body," said Landon, not turning. Reidel asked. "But why Marcus? Why not one of us?"

"I can only suggest theories," Mathis said, "but my presence may have had something to do with it, even through I was sick, and stunned, and not functioning. Maybe—it wouldn't try to transfer in my presence. We'll never know." But Reidel, white-faced, was recalling the moment when he had stood, in sweating terror, by Kester's body, frozen and numb. *If he had known.*

Landon motioned for silence, for the sight frame of the augmentator cleared and a face, weathered and bronzed beneath an odd peaked cap, peered from the screen.

—*Clannon. You are there?*

Landon felt he would burst with the surge of relief.

"*Use vocal speech, Vialmir.*" He touched an auxiliary control which would add sound transmission as well. Vialmir, in complete rapport with Landon and Mathis—for Landon had calibrated the augmentation beam to include him and Cleta too—had no trouble in expressing himself in any language they knew.

Landon turned to a middle-aged man with stars on his sleeve. "Will you talk to Vialmir, General? You don't have to speak aloud, but it's better if you do; you're no telepath, and it helps you focus your thoughts."

Hesitant, almost suspicious, the General came into the augmentation field, and Vialmir said from the screen, in clearly understandable English that mimicked the General's own accent, "You have captured the tool of the Rhu'inn? And you intend to set up this new device, the nullifier?"

"If we can, yes."

"Then you should know this," said Vialmir. "You have not been able to reach me, Clannon, because as soon as I touched the Rhu'inn I went into the telepathic trance for the total contact emergency relay to Galactic Central. I have instructions for you, Clannon. There was one ship in the sector, the *Transformation* of Vialles, and he was persuaded to come off course on the chance—"

Landon broke in with a wordless command below the perceptive level of the others.

—*No, don't tell them that!*

What good would it do to tell them that if the nullifier field could not be established, Earth would be moved to the list of Forbidden Stars? Shunned, permanently guarded—even the Watcher would be not allowed to communicate with the Federation? What good would it do, to tell them that in the case any spaceships leaving Earth would be destroyed, not allowed even to reach their own moon?

Vialmir said, "Of course, ordinarily, the *Transformation* could not land on a Closed Planet. He

would never be allowed to leave again. But if the
nullifier field can be established in time, he has
emergency permission to land. Would you care to
talk to the Commander? I can re-channel his sig-
nals for you."

Landon felt mildly stunned at this. It wasn't
luck, of course; this planet, though closed, was on
the regular trade routes, and at one time had been
a regular crossroads of the space lanes. All the
more reason it must be prevented from slipping
back to status of a Forbidden Star! If this system
were forbidden, it would mean costly re-
computing of all the star routes in this sector.

He explained, adding, "The Commander won't
be a telepath, perhaps, and he'll be communicating by voice, not rapport—"

Cleta said huskily, "Vialles is my home world.
Let me translate."

Gradually the augmentator picture altered. The
face of Vialmir, remained, a thin blurry frame, but
through and over it, another picture took shape, a
cabin filled with machinery that made the General lean forward and gasp. Vialmir was transmit-
ting, by developed kinetic telepathy, a picture
and a voice that were being received on his own
much more complex interspace receiver in the
Himalayas.

As Cleta dropped into the rapport, the Rim
Room of the *Transformation* and the face of a
elderly man with strong, aquiline features came
sharply into focus.

—*Commander Rivan. Who is communicating?*

Cleta spoke quickly in her own language;
Landon, free of the necessity of remaining so
deeply in rapport, translated the three-times-
relayed conversation. Cleta identified the *North-*

wind of Dvaneth, named and identified the seven
survivors, and finally broke contact to ask, "How
soon can the nullifier be set up?"

They conferred hastily. "About three days of
this planet's time," Mathis finally said and Cleta
translated it into sidereal units. The picture flickered in and out of focus, and finally Commander
Rivan said, "The *Transformation* is already behind schedule. However, in view of the pending
change in this Closed Planet's status, one way or
another—" Another pause while the focus flickered, dim to bright. "*If* the field can be established, we will come inside the magnetic field of
the planet and land a small shuttle—" He talked a
minute with someone out of sight range, finally
stipulating. "Provided, of course, the local authorities will guarantee suitably safeguarded
landing space."

Cleta translated and the General said hastily,
"Yes, yes, anything they ask."

Rivan continued "I'll try to get authority to
leave one or two volunteers on Earth, pending the
arrival of an official contact crew for the opening
of a planet. And we can take off the *Northwind*'s
survivors, if they're willing to be landed on Vialles." Cleta's wide eyes filled with tears. *To go
home!* All the time she was relaying the details of
landing arrangements, Reidel watched her, his
heart drenched in a flood of ice. Home—and his
dreams meant nothing in the face of that. As for
him, he'd see Dvaneth again, go into space again,
and some day when he was old, perhaps, someone
would ask about the time when he had been
spacewrecked on a Closed Planet. And by that
time it would be only an adventure story and
Cleta, only a memory.

He didn't wait to hear how the conference ended.

That night Landon and Mathis went into rapport for the purpose of translating the specifications for the nullifier field into Earth equivalents, and the equivalents into a workable blueprint. They began with only the General present, but within a few hours the place resembled a branch office of General Electric, with diagrams, wiring circuits, rejected components, and a jam of experts on power, communications and electronics.

Some things were identical and could be substituted; a vacuum tube is a vacuum tube and an electron stream is an electron stream and it doesn't matter how you measure or transmit it. Some could be improvised from existing equipment. Others were so strange that the consultants were baffled or, worse, derisive.

"If you can't understand it, how the hell are we supposed to?" demanded one of the young Army men reasonably. The General pointed at the augmentator.

"I don't understand that whozit, but I saw it work. I don't understand this one either, Mr. Briney, but I'm going to see it built. And you are going to build it, mister."

In the end their requisition list looked like an electrical supplies catalogue in three volumes. Landon stood on the steps with the General, watching young Briney drive away with it.

"This whole thing sounds preposterous, Landon. Will that starship commander really land on Earth?"

"If we get this field set up within his time limit, he will."

"If it's no important," the General said testily, "why put a time limit on it?"

"Even a few days will alter planetary positions at his destination, enough to waste a lot of fuel. A month's delay would alter his whole route enough to create real danger of collision with a planet or a star. His whole course would have to be re-computed, at a staggering loss of time and money. And he's not in the employ of the Federation, he's just a businessman, a trader. He could put in a claim for compensation insurance, but the Federation is just like any other bureaucracy, only bigger. There'd be years of red tape before he collected it, if he ever did."

"God above!" The General mopped his brow. "Bureaucracy. Business trips between stars!"

Eventually he came back to mundane matters. "Lawyers are battering the gate already with writs and so forth for the Marcus kid. We can't hold a civilian incommunicado indefinitely—and what in hell do we charge him with?"

Landon swore. "You could hold him if he had a contagious disease, couldn't you? Hang on to him—even if you have to give it out that he's dead." He reflected that was only anticipating the fact a little. A Rhu'inn host died when the Rhu'inn withdrew. Marcus' death sentence was in the nullifier. But then he had been under sentence of death all along.

Landon was too weary to sleep. Mathis, in the Base Hospital, was asleep under sedatives. In another room he found Steve Branzell, half-dressed, sitting up on the edge of his cot, and Landon had no words for his relief. If a lethally calibrated shocker missed a vital organ, it could paralyze permanently.

"Steve, I'm too tired to turn in, I'm going over and talk to the others. How about coming along, then?"

The women were finishing breakfast in an orderly, neat room when Branzell and Landon came in. Cleta rose and came to them, formally. "We've had no chance to thank you for all you've done, Watcher—"

"Landon," he corrected her gently. "And it's all right, that's my job. I'm sorry you have to be treated like prisoners, but it's for your own protection."

Linnit giggled. "I know. Even these women soldiers stare at us and try not to ask questions!"

"I feel like doing the same," Branzell said, with his warm laugh. "Aren't they marvelous, Landon? Why, they're children, they're hardly more than babies, and they've crossed the Galaxy!"

Dionie laid a light hand on Landon's arm. "Are Reidel and Arran going back with the *Transformation*?"

It had never occurred to Landon that they might not. Just as it had never occurred to him—until now—he too could go home, if he chose. No man who had touched a Closed Planet could return to infect a Galaxy forever watchful against Rhu'inn. But if Earth was to be opened, with the nullifier sweeping the planet clean as on open Federation worlds, then he, too, could return from the exile he had accepted as permanent!

"Can we see Arran and Reidel?" Linnit asked.

"I'm sorry. Not Arran at present. Reidel—"

"Reidel could come whenever he chose," Cleta interrupted. "Evidently he's decided, now we're safe, that we're not his problem any more!"

Landon felt perplexed, recalling Reidel's frantic anxiety when Cleta was not yet found. Suddenly he was overcome by fatigue. Liz saw it in his face and came to him, while Branzell was talking with the women.

"Go and rest while you can, Clint," she begged, and Landon drew her close and kissed her with hungry force.

"It will soon be over, darling. One way or the other."

"I'm frightened, Clint," she whispered. "I get blurry when I think of it all. I just have to—to remember that I love you, and forget the rest."

It was no time to suggest leaving Earth. He drew away, conscious of a break in the completeness of the group. "Where is Sylvia?" he demanded, and when no one answered, he said roughly, "Make sure she's here, somebody. We're not guarding you girls for the fun of it! Sylvia's the most vulnerable. I'd hate to have to lock her up—"

"It won't be necessary," said Dionie without moving. Cleta inclined her head slightly and when Landon listened he could hear Sylvia now, crying miserably. He met Branzell's accusing stare with a silent shake of his head; he was aware of her suffering, and he could do nothing to help. Branzell's high spirits, too, had been damped by the memory. They had lost Marcus—to something worse than death.

But it was worst for Sylvia. She had not had the training which made life endurable for such as Dionie. The situation would have been terrifying for any affectionate sister. For a hypersensitive empath, it was sheer hell.

Dionie followed Landon, when he left, and stood on the steps. She did not look like a child now. He supposed she was about fifteen by Earth reckoning, but all childishness had been stripped from her in the last few days.

"Do I have to go back to Dvaneth, Mr. Landon?"

He said gravely, "I've no authority to force you."

"There's no one, who'd miss me there, and nothing I can't have here, and—oh," she begged, "you do know, don't you?"

Landon nodded. He knew. An emotional triangle where two were telepath and empath was no fun for anyone. He wondered why Reidel didn't go to Alderbaran V where he could have them both, and hastily squelched that thought, glad that Dionie was empath and not telepath.

"Dionie, you can do me a favor," he said. "Sylvia hasn't had your training. Just help her live through the next few days. Whichever way things turn out, they're going to be rough."

He touched the white silky curls with his fingers, then walked away, not waiting for an answer, seeing that the weight of misery had already lightened in Dionie's great, too-wise eyes.

16

HE SLEPT and woke, dragged back to the conference room by the knowledge of the deadline. That jumble of confused parts and specifications must be somehow transformed into an apparatus which could protect a planet. It didn't have to be perfect. It just had to get going and stay going a while. There would be specialists on the *Transformation* who could make sure it would keep functioning properly. But unless they got it to work for a while, Rivan couldn't even land.

"If we're going to build this thing," Landon said, "I guess we'd better check and inventory all this junk." He picked up a list and started.

Evening came; midnight. Morning. The stacked jumble had somehow resolved itself into orderly process units. Landon put together each component, Briney tested it to be sure it would perform as desired, and Mathis checked the result against his mental blueprint. There were all too many rejections.

Once a hand dragging with fatigue brushed a bare wire and Landon was flung halfway across the room; he called a halt then, and made them all swallow food, coffee and benzedrine tablets. Landon and Reidel stumbled outside and sat on the steps to drink their coffee. The sun was just rising, and there was frost on the ground.

"You think we'll do it?"

"I don't know." Landon sagged. "If Briney wasn't so damn supercilious! If only I knew more about that resonator field. If only they had condensers that would take those confounded slow pulse vibrations!"

"I'm not much help," Reidel said. "If it were Arran—he worked in the Rim Room of a starship. He'd understand all this, if anyone could."

Landon re-entered the conference room as if it were purgatory, and Briney turned from a study of two slightly varying condensers. "We aren't going to do it in forty-eight hours, Landon. You're demanding impossible voltages, unless you put a whole high-tension system in here."

Landon straightened his shoulders and swore. "I want Arran down here!"

The General demurred. "You can have all the men you want, all the materials, all the consultants—"

"Damn it, we've got too many now! Mathis has had no technical education, and mine came before the nullifier was invented. Arran was trained in the Rim Room of a starship, and if he doesn't understand these things, nobody will and we might as well give up. We have no choice. We need him!"

In the end an apprehensive GI led Reidel through a steel corridor and unlocked a grating, and Arran, lying on a comfortless metal bunk, looked up bitterly.

"Are they locking you up too?"

"No, I came to get you out. Landon needs your help."

"He can go straight to—"

"He will, without you. What do you know about the nullifier?"

Arran gasped as if all the breath had been knocked out of him, and Reidel suddenly remembered that Arran knew nothing at all, not even about Marcus' danger. He had been told nothing, simply locked up. He explained quickly in their own language; Arran was looking sick.

"They don't have nullifiers on starships, they only work within the magnetic field of a planet. I've heard about them, but I don't know much. It's lucky I didn't! Being with Marcus so long—" His face was so white that Reidel thought he would fall over. He steadied the youngster with his arm.

"I'm all right. It was only— Is he safely locked up?"

Reidel reassured him, and Arran relaxed slightly. "Of course that's why only telepaths are allowed to know the specifications, until they're actually in construction. But if they're building a null-field here, it means the planet's not closed any more, it means—" His voice caught.

"Sooner than you think, Arran. There's a ship in orbit now, and if we can establish the field, he'll land, and take anyone off who wants to go home."

Arran swallowed. "I'd call that an incentive!"

Landon's hunch had been a good one. Arran, though he did not understand the nullifier, was familiar with the special resonators that had baffled them, and with other devices invented since Landon's training days.

But it was still a heartbreaking job, racing against a growing conviction that it would never be finished.

Evening came again and night, and Landon called a halt when Mathis dropped a delicate tube—the only one of its kind in the state—and only a miracle picked it up unbroken.

He went out on the steps again, letting the night wind hit him in the face; he forced down another benzedrine tablet and a cup of black coffee. Arran said behind him, "Think we'll make the deadline?"

"Hell with the deadline." Landon would have liked to stretch out for a catnap, but he knew if he shut his eyes, he'd sleep for a week. "If Rivan won't wait it out, let him go on."

"No!" Arran's voice rose into violence. "If the ship can't land, what use is this?"

Landon swore. "If the planet's open, there will be other ships. If it stays closed, you'll never go home."

Mathis' footsteps were so quiet neither man had heard him come out on the porch. "If the *Transformation* can't land, you'll have to live here, so don't be temperamental. The important thing is to get the field working before Marcus does something to stop us. Let's go back in. We'll wire it all together and hope for the best.

Morning brightened to noon. Then, without any special feeling of achievement, Landon tightened a final screw and stepped back. The incredible makeshift tangle covered the whole wall.

". . . think that's got it."

"Damnedest mess I ever saw." Briney was almost asleep where he stood. "Never take any prizes for design, that's for sure."

They stared, bleary eyed with fatigue, at the insane conglomeration of wires, meters, dials and makeshifts which had no names or comprehensible functions in Earth science. Arran said with a face-splitting yawn, "Will it *work*?"

Mathis groaned. "The power sources all work, but I've got to make the final tests on the telepath bands."

"You'd better rest first."

"Later. I couldn't relax now. Did we make the deadline?"

Landon looked at the clock. It had lost its power to torment him, and was just a clock again. He rubbed his eyes to make sure they were not deceiving him, and looked again.

"With about four hours to spare."

Mathis stood before it, abstracted and intent. "Throw each switch in turn, but don't turn on the main field till I have each circuit adjusted separately for compensating resonances on the telepath frequencies, or the sonic exciters will blow the whole thing out. And we'll have it all to do over again."

"Don't even *say* that," Briney groaned.

It was really nerve-racking work now. Each sector hummed briefly with screaming vibration. Subsonics made them moan with undefined malaise. Landon made some minor blunder, and the telempath, now under doubled strain—physical exhaustion and the tortuous telepathic work to be done—finally snapped.

"Damn it, get out, get out!" His tormented face was white. "How can I tune this with you all screaming at me?"

"I haven't said a word," Briney protested unwisely, and Mathis turned on him, raging.

"You're a head-blind imbecile who doesn't even know when he's broadcasting his own ignorance! Get out! Get out! I can't compensate for all your stupidities! Get out and leave me alone!" Mathis was screaming now, his small twisted body twitching, his face drawn and white. Briney backed off in horror. Landon turned, shoving the others out before him, and in the hallway he said to Briney, "No, he's not crazy. You can't imagine the strain he's been under."

"I guess I can, a little. Toward the end, I could hear you fellows thinking." Tired as he was, Briney was scientist enough to look at Landon in wondering surmise. Landon laid a hand on his shoulder.

"I've seen surgical crews use rudimentary telepathy without realizing it. All good team workers do. You're a damn good latent telepath, youngster, and if this goes through, you'll get proper training." He gave the young man a gentle shove. "Go crawl in the sack, we're through."

Arran stumbled and swore. "If anyone had told me I'd ever see a null-field built in three days, I'd have called him a congenital liar. Damned if I like it, though, leaving old Mathis all by himself, he's out on his feet. I'm going back—"

Reidel started out of a sleepwalking daze. "I'll—go."

"If you don't trust me—" Arran began resentfully.

Landon knew this was the time to put confidence in Arran, or lose him forever. Just now, he was one of them again. "You go, Arran. Mathis would choke me or Reidel, either. He's not sore at you just now."

Returning, Arran saw Mathis and hesitated.

Mathis was all right in there alone, and Mathis had thrown them out. Why should he risk a rebuff. He almost turned away.

Then—

No one ever knew how it happened. A guard was to be court-martialed and babble of hypnotism, but that did not explain how human flesh and blood escaped steel bars. Arran saw only the heavy Army pistol, raised toward the absorbed, unsuspecting back of the telempath. Drugged with fatigue, he did not even recognize Ned Marcus. He simply flung himself on the gun arm, dragging it down.

He knew nothing about guns. If he thought of the weapon at all, he thought of one like the shocker, and the roar and the blow that struck low in the chest reeled him back only momentarily. There was no immediate pain, and he hung on grimly, his hands locked on Marcus' throat. Even at the edge of exhaustion, there had been a final spurt of strength in Arran.

He felt the weight sink away. The gun lay harmless. He did not hear Mathis shouting; he did not hear the vibration die out and scream noiselessly up into complete silence, nor feel the tiny sting as the null-field flickered permanently into the spaces between atoms, setting up resonances that would reverberate all through the Earth and its atmosphere. He heard only a ringing in his ears. He hit the floor and blacked out.

Landon had been the first to hear the shots, but by the time he raced back along the corridor, Mathis was already bending over the two young bodies sprawled so close together. Marcus was still twitching a little. He opened pain-glazed, dying eyes.

"Nullifier on . . . fools . . . Earth's last chance . . . real glory . . . gone," he gasped, and his eyes rolled back and stared at something between the atoms of the world.

Now there were shouts everywhere and running feet; a crowd was collecting fast, but it was a minute or two before they realized Arran was still alive.

Landon shouted, "Get a doctor, somebody," and knelt beside the boy. Mathis said, with soft finality, "Too late, Clannon. Too close to the heart."

Arran was conscious now, just barely. He muttered something about noise on the Rim, then his eyes cleared and he said in a hoarse hurting voice, "Reidel—"

Reidel slid his arm under the boy's neck, and his face was gray with grief and guilt. "I should have gone back with you—"

"Always—worryin' about us." Arran's head rested on Reidel's knees. He said through bloody spit, "Wanted to say—Cleta never gave a damn for me—I was—"

"Don't try to talk. It's all right, son," Reidel whispered, holding his hand.

"Why did you call me—son?" Arran suddenly was not breathing any more. He coughed, a great cough that seemed to tear his chest loose, drowning in his own blood, and died.

Reidel stumbled away from his side, blind with tears, and Landon took him by the arm and guided him into a small private office. He shoved him into a chair and Reidel leaned his face in his hands, torn with straining sobs. Landon knew it was more than the death of a friend; it was the breakdown that had been pending since the

Northwind came apart in space and Reidel found himself responsible for six strangers. Landon stood there and sweated it out, suffering with Reidel and not able to help. Then Cleta was there and she was crying in Reidel's arms and Landon tiptoed out and left them alone.

"He was the only one of us who was going home," Cleta wept, "and now he'll never go."

It was not for some time that Reidel would realize exactly what she said; that she had never meant to leave him. But they needed no words to know that they would never again leave the world where they had found each other.

Landon, more than anyone else, was most heavily burdened by the horrible death of the two boys. He thought of Branzell, of Sylvia. Of course no sacrifice was too great to stop the Rhu'inn; but that was little comfort now.

"If only they hadn't been so damned young!"

He said what Cleta had said, kneeling by the two lifeless bodies. "Poor little devil, he wanted to go home. And now he'll never go."

Mathis turned, and his twisted face was gentle for once. "But we have the nullifier," he said, "and the planet's open. Arran hated this world, and he didn't love any of us. But he was the one who gave it to us. Look, Watcher. Out the window."

Landon looked through the light, soft-falling flakes of the winter's first snow. For the first time in twenty thousand years, a great silver ship from the stars was circling and dropping gently to the surface of the Closed Planet—closed no more.

ANDRE NORTON

Witch World Series

Enter the Witch World for a feast of adventure and enchantment, magic and sorcery.

89705	**Witch World**	$1.95
87875	**Web of the Witch World**	$1.95
80805	**Three Against the Witch World**	$1.95
87323	**Warlock of the Witch World**	$1.95
77555	**Sorceress of the Witch World**	$1.95
94254	**Year of the Unicorn**	$1.95
82356	**Trey of Swords**	$1.95
95490	**Zarsthor's Bane** (illustrated)	$1.95

Ursula K. Le Guin

10705	**City of Illusion** $2.25	
47806	**Left Hand of Darkness** $2.25	
66956	**Planet of Exile** $1.95	
73294	**Rocannon's World** $1.95	

Available wherever paperbacks are sold or use this coupon

ACE SCIENCE FICTION
P.O. Box 400, Kirkwood, N.Y. 13795

POUL ANDERSON

78657	**A Stone in Heaven**	$2.50
20724	**Ensign Flandry**	$1.95
48923	**The Long Way Home**	$1.95
51904	**The Man Who Counts**	$1.95
57451	**The Night Face**	$1.95
65954	**The Peregrine**	$1.95
91706	**World Without Stars**	$1.50

Available wherever paperbacks are sold or use this coupon